PRAISE FOR
THE SHADOW GALAXY

"A sharply entertaining collection spanning all corners of the genre, filled with horrors and wonders and acutely human moments." —Adrian Tchaikovsky, author of *Children of Memory*

"*The Shadow Galaxy* is a mind-blowing collection of weird, fun, dark, wild, character-driven tales by a powerful new voice! J. Dianne Dotson's star is rising! Highly recommended!" —Jonathan Maberry, *New York Times* bestselling author of *Kagen the Damned* and *V-Wars*

"These stories are as lyrical, uplifting, otherworldly and unsettling as any faerie tale, and demonstrate Dotson's ability to write confidently across a wide range of genres, including fantasy, science fiction, and horror." — Gareth L. Powell, author of *Stars and Bones*

"A deeply satisfying collection of fantasies that ranges from Americana to outer space, charming and precise in equal measure." —Paul Cornell, author of *Witches of Lychford* and *I Walk with Monsters*

"There truly is a story for everyone in this collection of stories. If you haven't found one yet, then keep reading!" —Blaise Ancona, Under the Radar SFF Books

"Dotson keeps these unsettling, eerie, and occasionally full-on horrifying tales short and punchy" —*Publishers Weekly*

J. DIANNE DOTSON

THE
SHADOW
GALAXY

A COLLECTION OF SHORT STORIES AND POETRY

TREPIDATIO
PUBLISHING

ISBN: 978-1-68510-068-1 (sc)
ISBN: 978-1-68510-069-8 (ebook)
Library of Congress Catalog Number: 2022947660

First printing edition: March 3, 2023
Printed by Trepidatio Publishing in the United States of America.
Edited by Sean Leonard
Proofreading and Interior Layout by Scarlett R. Algee

Trepidatio Publishing, an imprint of JournalStone Publishing
3205 Sassafras Trail
Carbondale, Illinois 62901

Trepidatio books may be ordered through booksellers or by contacting:
JournalStone | www.journalstone.com

For my sons, Daniel and Allen, my bright stars.
For my beloved Gareth, for your constant love and support.

CONTENTS

INTO THE DARKEST HOLLOW: TALES OF HORROR

LOVE AND OTHER MOMENTS: TRACES OF THE HEART

FAR APPALACHIA: TALES FROM THE ANCIENT MOUNTAINS

RESONANT THOUGHTS: SOME POETRY

THE SHADOW GALAXY

A COLLECTION OF SHORT STORIES AND POETRY

SHADOW SHORES
TALES FROM THE SEA

ONE EVENING IN FOGVALE

Miranda Mirthwick watched as the fog billowed over the point, engulfing the light which cast its feeble beam to the northwest. Soon the cloud curled over in a slow wave, combed by windswept trees along the high ridge.

"Gonna be a thick one tonight!" her grandfather bellowed, and then he murmured over a paper he crinkled in his weathered hands.

"I'll put the kettle on, Grandfather," Miranda replied. And she set to work at their small stove.

A low, deep groan heralded the sound of a very tired foghorn in the bay.

Miranda had daydreamed of an evening stroll along the little winding stone path along the bay. Grandfather would have joined her on a clear night, and she happily would have matched his halting pace. But he was firmly ensconced tonight, and doubly so, the moment she handed him an earthenware mug of tea.

"Do you know, I might just have my walk," Miranda said, thinking aloud.

Grandfather harrumphed. "In *this* pea soup?"

"Aye, the very same," Miranda said with a smile, and she took off her apron, hung it on the peg by the door, and in turn grabbed her long coat.

"Don't be slipping on the rocks, mind," Grandfather cautioned her. "And be back before the fire's out! I'm feeling the chill tonight, and my bones are a bit stiff."

"I will, Grandfather," Miranda reassured him, and she gave him a delicate kiss on his balding head.

She swept out the door, and soon realized her grandfather had been quite correct. It was indeed a "pea soup" kind of a night. She kept along the stone path, and the gas lamps sputtered and flickered. Miranda knew the path well, and so she knew where to step carefully.

The walk excited her. She had been inside much of the day, working on a quilt between reading and writing poetry. She would alternate between the three, and then prepared an early supper for herself and her grandfather. It was a lonely life sometimes, but other times, she was glad to be out here. Her grandfather had sailed for many years, and now he was retired, and she lived with him full-time to look after him.

It meant that she had to carve out social time with others her age, but this she found unsatisfying.

She sighed as she walked along the path. She watched her pointed toes, dark angles in the foggy night. One before the other, never hasty, only measured and careful. Her friends might call her the same.

By and by she heard more foghorns across the bay, as if old spirits called to each other. She wondered what they might be saying. She heard the distant clanging of a bell somewhere. And all the time, the soft slapping of low waves as the bay met the pebbled shore.

Her coat and hat-covered hair quickly filled with droplets from the fog, which muffled the sounds of everything around her. But she paused and tilted her head, and her damp braid fell forward.

There is music somewhere… she thought. *Beautiful, angelic music!*

And it grew louder. She kept walking and wondered where it could be coming from. There were no fancy houses in this part of the bay. They all faced the open sea, whereas she and her grandfather lived just down from the point, shielded from the ocean view. In clear weather, they could see across the bay to the towns on the other side; they would be twinkling tonight. But the fog hid that familiar sight from her.

The music swelled, and became more resonant, and she felt it move her as her eyes watered. Something like a cello thrummed, but it was not quite the same. And then she heard…but surely not! Someone called to her in song, "Miranda, Miranda!"

She froze. The song rose and fell and swooped with its strange instruments. She heard them clearly yet could not understand them. She could only feel their beauty.

Perhaps I imagined it.

But again, someone cried, "Miranda! Miranda!" And this time, the voice added, "Miranda Mirthwick, you are cordially invited to join us!"

And she blinked, and the fog opened to reveal a house with golden light streaming from all its windows.

Whose house is that? Miranda wondered. *Have I gone astray, and I'm in another neighborhood? I have not been careful!*

She saw figures on the lawn, dancers twirling, and someone on long legs strode down the walk with arms outstretched toward her.

"Miranda!" the person cried. She remained still.

Figures brushed past her, and she gasped, as lords and ladies stepped along the path, out of the fog and toward the light of the house, and on their arms were draped ropes of twinkling lights. The gowns of the ladies glowed like lamps from within. Miranda felt dizzy. But she did not move.

Finally, the tall figure approached her, and it was a man. Or perhaps not? It was a tall figure, in every respect like a young man, but whose face and eyes seemed to shift, disguising his age. His hair was long and light brown, his forehead high, his eyebrows angled, and his cheekbones sharp. His eyes were grey-green like the Atlantic, and when he smiled, Miranda forgot time and place…and manners as well.

He stepped before her and bowed low.

"I am Arden Blake," the man said…if man he was. "We have been waiting for you!"

Miranda knew not what else to do, so she curtsied in politeness and said, "Thank you. I am—well, I suppose you know my first name, Miranda—"

"Mirthwick," answered Arden, with a smile too kind to Miranda's eyes. "We know of you! And we are so happy you have come to us at last."

Miranda stared at him, and then shivered at her own rudeness. "He-hello, Mr. Blake," she answered, and she took his hand. She felt self-conscious that her own hand felt clammy, yet his was warm and dry. She realized then that not only was he warm and dry, but the great house behind him, into which streamed all manner of guests, was brilliantly lit and untouched by fog at all. And above the house the stars shown as flickering pinpoints, and she traced the shape of a constellation she did not know.

"Mr. Blake," she began.

"Please, do call me Arden," said the man. The air around him seemed to warp, as if an illusion from heat.

"Ar-Arden," Miranda stammered. "How do you know me, Arden?"

Arden laughed, clear and jolly, and others in the dancing crowd heard him, and exclaimed, "Ah!" or laughed joyfully with him.

"We have always known you here. You have walked by us many times, but never stopped until tonight. Welcome to Fogvale!"

Miranda turned around. She could see a blank expanse, a fog bank, just behind her. She looked toward the bay, and it was wreathed in fog as well. But a few boats approached from the dark water, and they were all lit with garlands of lights and flowers.

"I—I don't know of a place called Fogvale," Miranda answered, doubtful, yet mesmerized.

Arden laughed again. "Well, you've arrived in it, finally, and so you must visit properly! We are having a grand ball tonight. Would you be so kind as to join us?"

And Arden held out his arm. The clicking of boots and heels met Miranda's ears, and yet the sounds were still lost, as if she were still inside the fog as she had been before.

The house beckoned, and the strange and drifting music charmed her. So she took Arden's arm, but she said, "I cannot stay long, I must be back home to tend my grandfather."

Arden nodded his handsome, sharp head, and said, "Of course, of course. For now, refreshments, and dancing! For it is truly an honor to find you here."

Miranda wanted to ask many questions, but her eyes and ears were inundated with such beauty that she could not form the words.

Which is odd, considering I am a poet!

Miranda took Arden's offered arm, and he gazed down at her with half-lidded eyes. In their pupils, she thought she saw a deep light. And for a moment, she felt as though she were falling…falling into the depths of those pupils, falling toward a cold and distant light. She jerked, as if awakening from a dream of falling, and he laughed softly down at her.

"Take good care, Miss Mirthwick! The steps are steep, and the mist from the fog might make you slip."

She knew, though, that the steps had nothing to do with what she had felt. And her head felt a bit heavy, but she focused on the shimmering entrance to the great house. As multi-colored skirts brushed past her, the voices of everyone intermingled with music from within the manor. Scents wafted past her too, fragrances from flowers of faraway lands that she had never visited. As she stood at the doorway, one lady turned and her skirts swirled as she did so, and she looked directly into Miranda's eyes.

The lady's own eyes were deep indigo, almost violet, and her creamy neck shone beneath a coiled updo of raven-hued hair, just as iridescent as that bird's feathers might be. The dark night-eyes lowered their long, black eyelashes just a bit, and the lady smiled from her cupid's bow lips to reveal small but perfect teeth. Deep in those eyes, just as with Arden's, something shown.

The lady outstretched a delicate hand sheathed in a long, white silk glove. Dizzy, Miranda looked down at the woman's cobalt blue dress, noticing many thousands of stones glinting in its folds. She marveled.

She started when the lady said, "Miss Mirthwick, darling," in a deep, velvety voice, almost a purr. "Long have we waited, dear heart. Do come in."

Miranda's feeling of vertigo increased, and she fell forward just a bit, but caught the woman's gloved hand and held it firmly. The woman then pulled her gently, and Miranda stepped forward into the home.

The door closed behind her. Not as a door normally might. Miranda was simply inside, when before she was outside. There was no active closing that she could see or remember. She felt a tiny spark of fear at the base of her neck. Her legs trembled, and she looked down at her dew-covered, dark and simple gown, and then up at something quite spectacular.

It was a vast hall of white and gold and silver, its ceiling like a great cathedral arching up above and out of sight. She realized, suddenly, that she could not even decipher a true ceiling. She felt dizzy again. The lady held her hand fast, her smile never wavered.

"You've entered our realm now," the lady said. Miranda looked down at her, for now she realized the woman was half a head shorter in stature.

"What—what is this place?" stammered Miranda.

Arden, who had been conversing with other guests, swept over and bowed. "My Lady Giltovar!" he said to the violet-eyed lady. "I see you have officially met our Miss Mirthwick and guided her in. How thoughtful!"

The two gazed at each other as if across an infinite chasm. Miranda, innocent though she was in many respects, could see a flash of recognition between them that did not read to her as one of kindness. But she admitted to herself that both were quite beautiful. She wondered how old they must be. And then she turned her head to look at the others in the hall.

She could see musicians playing harps and stringed instruments she did not recognize. She heard the lilting voices of a distant choir but did not see who sang among it. All about her, gowned ladies strode, some of them hand in hand, others holding the hands of gentlemen. Some of the gentlemen held the hands of other gentlemen. And some individuals possessed an undefinable sensibility, clothed in suits or gowns or lavish togas and sarongs. One personage clad in white and gold emerged among the guests, who parted to make way for them.

The person bore pale hair in silver, gold, and copper streaks, and their ears were lined with ruby earrings. Their eyes were large and dark brown, nearly black, and their mouth was small and tidy. The air around this person wavered, much as Miranda had witnessed before: as if from a mirage.

In a low voice, the person spoke: "Lady Mirthwick, it is an honor." The tall form bowed and extended a hand as it glided over to her…or that is how it seemed to Miranda, so smooth was their movement. She found herself taking the hand and curtsying, and the air around this person shimmered and sparkled like so many fireflies winking on and off, spinning in a pattern. These tiny sparkles captured the deep red of the ruby earrings. Miranda's vision swam in all the glinting of light. But the person seemed to know this, and so held firmly to her hand, but gently, and fixed her with their onyx eyes.

"Long have we awaited your presence. I am Tivoxxan. Welcome to my humble estate."

Upon hearing "humble," a tickling sort of laugh bubbled up inside Miranda's throat, and it escaped before she could stop it, so she nearly hiccupped in embarrassment and gently covered her mouth with her other hand.

"I am honored, Tivoxxan," she said breathlessly, her cheeks scarlet. Something about the rich yet subtle scent of this person and their mesmerizing, deep eyes made her feel flustered, and not in an entirely unpleasant way.

"Would you," Tivoxxan murmured, "join me in a dance?"

Miranda looked down at her shabby dress, her faded wool coat, and the scuffed toes of her laced boots. But Tivoxxan dipped their head to capture her gaze again, and she forgot her workaday clothing, and indeed nearly everything else, and said, "Yes."

And so, they whirled, among the many gilded and bejeweled skirts, in the scented haze of sparkle and lamplight and music and mystic airs. Miranda felt giddy, and she laughed in pleasure from the pristine dancing of Tivoxxan, whose firm hands guided her smoothly about the great house.

Tivoxxan led her, dancing all the while, to an exquisite alcove that faced a door. Bowing, Tivoxxan released her, and opened the door. Miranda peered in and gasped at what she beheld.

Beyond the door, an immense, unimaginable space existed, filled with extraordinary objects. She could not name most of them, though she recognized chariots and wagons. One looked like a great wood and canvas bird, with two layers of wings and blades on its beak. Near its beak, a maple leaf emblem shone. Another object, larger, shone in a deep slate grey, chiseled in many angles, and it hung suspended in the air. Tivoxxan eyed her and slowly closed their eyes until they were mere slits.

"Another time," Tivoxxan murmured, pulling the door closed.

"What—what were all those?" stammered Miranda, her mind struggling to understand.

"A collection," Tivoxxan replied, pointy chin dipping, dark eyes locked with hers.

Miranda's hands had fallen to her sides, and she felt a hard lump, and realized it was a pocket watch her grandfather had given her. She reached for it and opened it up. She stared at it.

"My watch has stopped," she said softly. She looked up at Tivoxxan, which gave her a thrill, and asked, "Do you know the time?"

"I know time," Tivoxxan said, a tiny smirk at the corner of their mouth. "It does not matter much to us here."

Miranda squinted up at Tivoxxan.

"Perhaps not," she said, "but I must get back to Grandfather. It is late, and he does not know where I am."

"I daresay he does not," Tivoxxan answered evenly, the metallic-hued hair falling forward just a bit.

Miranda stepped back and glanced about. Arden and Lady Giltovar watched keenly close by. Music played on, undulating, some of it by stringed instruments, the rest by sounds Miranda could not recognize. The dancers bobbed, like great blossoms in a breeze. Miranda felt herself shudder.

"I must go," she said suddenly, and she turned, but Tivoxxan caught her by the elbow.

"Lady Mirthwick," Tivoxxan said, voice honeyed, deep, sweet, and enchanting, "would you stay? We can bring dear Grandfather here. He has ventured this way before, but never found the entry."

Miranda stared at Tivoxxan with eyes wide open. "I—no. No, thank you so very much. Grandfather has a home. Our home."

Arden and Lady Giltovar approached them.

"We would like very much for you to stay, Miss Mirthwick," Arden told her.

The Lady said, "Quite! You mustn't go. We have much to show you! You have only glimpsed a portion of our home."

Tivoxxan raised a hand. "Thank you, that will do, dear friends. I will escort Lady Mirthwick to the door."

Lady Giltovar stepped forth, her fascinator shivering in peacock-hued baubles, and said, sharply, "We have brought her within. And so, she must remain."

Arden added, "We have our rules."

Tivoxxan looked at each of them in turn, down a long and slender, pointy nose.

"I have my own rules," Tivoxxan declared. "Miranda Mirthwick displays a duty of care. We would do well to honor this." Turning to her, Tivoxxan then said, "You are not quite ready. That much is clear. But one day you shall be, and I will guide your return here. I have much more to share with you. And we can help you."

Miranda felt a pang of angst, for a great part of her dearly wanted to stay. She wanted to explore behind that doorway again. She wanted to go into the many doorways she could now see all about the room. She wanted to know. She wanted to *feel*. But Grandfather waited.

Tivoxxan took her hand gently and drew her to the entrance. A sigh rippled among the guests as she approached the great door, open into the night again, and Tivoxxan stood with her at the threshold.

"May I?" asked Tivoxxan, leaning toward her a bit.

"May you…what?" Miranda asked, breaking into a sweat.

"I have a gift for you. A kiss upon your brow."

Miranda stared into the dark eyes of Tivoxxan, and wished with all her might she could stay, but she did not want to worry Grandfather any more.

"You may," she whispered. Tivoxxan bent and softly kissed her forehead. She felt a tingling sensation where those lips caressed her, and it coursed all through her body. She felt suddenly very awake, and keen, and every sense felt sharp.

"For when you are ready," said Tivoxxan. "Good night, Lady Mirthwick, and many blessings to you."

Miranda glanced behind Tivoxxan and witnessed Arden and Lady Giltovar scowling beyond. She wondered for a moment, but some instinct told her to go, and go quickly. She squeezed Tivoxxan's hands and dashed down the broad steps to the promenade along the water. She turned back to wave or thank them and found nothing but the fog. No lights, no great house, nothing.

"Oh!" she cried, and she felt tears sting her eyes. "Oh, no, please! I wanted it to be real. I wanted to stay!"

But her forehead still tingled. She touched it with her fingertips. Then she felt for her pocket watch. It ticked steadily.

"It's working again," she whispered. She looked behind her. Still nothing. A buoy in the dark water clanged, and the water slapped along the rocky shore, as ever. But other than these sounds, she was met with absolute quiet. She broke that peace with the sound of her heels clicking on stone as she paced quickly back toward the old house.

It took both a long and a short time for Miranda to get there, and her body shook with unexpected emotion when she saw the creamy light of a lantern in the window. *Home*, she thought, but now she felt doubtful.

She stopped at the door and turned to look behind her. The fog had lifted, and stars sparkled overhead. Where had she been? *And when have I been?* But she felt exhausted just by thinking that and let her mind and her fatigue work through the current moment. She took her old key out of her coat pocket and turned the lock. She entered the warmth of the home she had known for so long and shut out the strange night.

Her grandfather snored in his chair, his spectacles slipping down his nose, an open book rising and falling on his bulbous belly. She hated to wake him, and yet…

"Grandfather," she called softly.

He snorted, shifted, adjusted his spectacles, and the book fell to the floor. She walked over and picked it up for him.

"Ah! Thank you, my dear," he said, clearing his throat. "Must've dozed off. Did you have a nice walk?"

Miranda sat next to him and stared at him and felt her eyes water.

"Yes," she said, "but I missed you."

He looked at her through his glasses, and then his forehead crinkled. He took them off, wiped them with a kerchief, and put them back on to look again.

"What's that on your forehead, Miranda?" he asked.

She felt a jolt, almost electrical, shoot through her.

"I…I don't know," she lied, and she rose and walked to their old mirror. Her reflection showed a young woman rosy of cheek, and a brow with a sparkling little mark on her forehead. She rubbed at it, and it disappeared. For some reason, this made her feel sad.

"Grandfather," she said slowly, "what was it like here, long ago? Were there mansions along the quay?"

Grandfather chuckled. "Ah, things were different then, dear girl. We had a lot of visitors that would come and go with the seasons. Great houses, great parties."

Miranda's heart pounded. "Did you ever go?"

"Nay, that was when I was a lad, and my mum told me never to walk along the quay during the party season," he recalled, his eyes glazing over.

"Did you ever…did you ever see anything…unusual?" she pressed, tense.

"Well, there was that one time," said Grandfather, rubbing his wiry, grey chin. "There was a great schooner, came in one night, I remember it clear as day. Covered in lanterns. And everywhere else, a thick fog."

Miranda sat next to him again and gripped the arms of her chair. "Did—did you see anyone in it?"

Her grandfather blinked and shook his head. "Nay, but I remember the lights. Made you dizzy to look at them. Always assumed it was headed for the party houses."

"And did you ever see it again?" Miranda asked, her mouth dry.

Grandfather again shook his head, and he smiled at her. "Nay, dear girl. Could have been a dream, you know. That was a long time ago."

"I wonder," she couldn't help but say.

"You keep wondering, sweet Miranda," said Grandfather. "Never stop wondering."

Miranda touched her forehead. Then she stood, and leaned over him, and kissed him on the cheek. "Good night, Grandfather."

"Dream well," he answered her.

"I shall," she said over her shoulder, as she walked up the narrow, creaking stairs to her bedroom. When she closed her eyes, she could hear music, and feel an arm about her waist, and see lights twinkling, and a great bird flying over a distant land, in some other time, in some other place, into a fog.

THE NIGHT OF LONGSHANKS

Ten plastic owls bobbed like gaudy jewels along a string in the warm night. Lanterns set bouncing by errant puffs of breeze that, given enough time, would build into a gale as a storm swilled off the cape. Jeddy wiped her chin, sticky from melted cherry popsicle juice. Her toes wriggled in the sand, still warm despite the darkness. The wind rose a bit more, and the chimes of a mobile home tinkled.

"They say," Grandma's voice crackled, "that on a night like this in 1794, the pirate Wolfgang Longshanks sent a schooner down the cape, wind filling its sails like the chest of a banty rooster. He weren't on the ship hisself; but he told the crew to swoop in with torches and set the encampments alight right out there, right at the edge of that spit. Burnt them all while they slept."

Jeddy shivered. It was a likeable feeling, hearing a ghost story on a dark beach at night. She tried to imagine that this ramshackle collection of campers, tents, and more permanent mobile homes known as Pine Beach Woods Campground might once have been the site of a gruesome massacre. She'd heard of Pirate Longshanks before, but thought it was just another beach legend. And the only thing that seemed remarkable nowadays were the owl string lights, in yellow, green, and red, as they swung glowing, almost taunting her with their great plastic eyes from across the sandy alley.

"You're gettin' sleepy," said Grandma. "Let's get you to bed."

Jeddy didn't want to go in. She would have preferred to sleep under the open sky, flickering with stars awash with fast-moving clouds. She listened and could hear a buoy out in the black water, beyond the moan and crash of the waves. The wind had indeed picked up now. The pines sighed and bent, and the owl lights danced.

And besides, the camper smelled of mildew and ancient coffee. Jeddy didn't like sleeping in it, and it was cramped even for a young girl like herself. There was a table that converted to a bed, and a bigger bed in the rear of the trailer. She had to take the bed table, with its stiff cushion covered by an old sheet, and she hated it. She wanted her giant daisy-patterned sleeping bag right out on the sand.

"Crabs'll gitchye," said Grandpa, wriggling his fingers at her, as if reading her thoughts.

She squeaked, indulging him, and he laughed.

Grandma pursed her lips and looked at the sky.

"Well, if the crabs don't," she said, "the rain will, here in a couple hours. I can smell it."

Jeddy sighed and planted herself in the camping chair outside the door. Grandpa brought her a beach towel, which smelled like sunscreen and damp sand and a bit of mold. She tucked it around herself, refusing to go into the camper. He spoke in a low voice to Grandma, and they both went inside, leaving the door open.

Shifting in the camp chair so that she curled up with her legs on the seat, she watched the owl lights, and the wind whistled more, and she became drowsy. Then she jerked, realizing she'd at some point fallen asleep, and she felt sticky and sandy. Her tongue stuck to the roof of her mouth, and she dislodged it and disliked the taste. She looked across where the owl lights had hung at the camper across the way, and she sat up straight. The lights were off.

She reasoned they had probably just been unplugged. But a quick look down at the public bathrooms, usually lit from above by a streetlamp, told her the power was out at the campground. The wind funneled from the sea and into the pines, and the only other sound was that of windchimes. Even the buoy had gone silent.

She stood up, and her feet tingled, for she had been sitting for so long they had fallen asleep. She danced where she stood, and then something caught her eye. She turned and looked far to her left, out where a little stream ran to the sea, and a pale light shone on that water. The moon had arisen and sparkled on its surface. But following that little thread of water, her eyes found more light…and it was not electronic, and it was not the moon, nor the stars. They were little flames, rising and falling, ten of them, all in a line.

She swallowed, then tried to cry out for her grandparents, but she could make no sound. Some dark and silent host marched from the sea, bearing torches.

Longshanks! she thought in a panic.

She turned to enter the camper behind her, only to find the door both shut and locked. Her lips began to quiver. Her grandparents would never have locked her out. With a small whine, she turned, and then beheld the torches advancing, and she made a decision.

I will not run.

She would face this dread throng and its dread leader, Wolfgang Longshanks. For at their head marched a dark figure, taller than the others, limping, with a great hat. She could barely see its outline. The sand shuffled behind him, where the ten pirates with their ten torches followed.

But this was no ordinary fire they carried: the torches did glow, but they were muted, pale tufts of eerie light, as if seen under glass and then again underwater. They more resembled phosphorescent light than any fire. And as the pirates marched toward her, she could not discern them well. They were outlines of pirates, but not at all living flesh.

Still she stood, shuddering, for she knew they would come to her. And indeed, their leader marched right up to her, and she found herself looking up and up, and into eyes the same pale tinge as the torches behind him, but she could not make out any other features in his face in the darkness.

"An' who might you be, lass?" a low hissing voice asked her from under that great, billowing hat.

"Just…just Jeddy," she stammered. She looked right and left, and no one else could be seen…no one alive, anyway.

"Just Jeddy," answered Longshanks, "do yer know who I am, lass?"

Jeddy nodded. "You're the pirate, Wolfgang Longshanks!"

"Aye," his quiet, low voice answered. The wind seemed to shift his image, making him flicker as much as the torches in his host.

"An' do ye know, Jeddy-lass," continued the pirate, "what we be doin' here, at this beachhead, on this night?"

Jeddy swallowed with a very dry mouth and considered. "This was the night, wasn't it? You lit all those fires, long ago."

"Aye," said Longshanks. "Aye," and the latter word came out like a long sigh. "Drunk upon the rum, eyes on revenge, I sent the lads down to torch them all. And so damned us all. So here we be, set to wander here always, in the dark, and marchin' along the same path, over and over, as the years roll by, until the sea takes the land, and then we'll be marchin' beneath the waves yet, for all time."

Jeddy tried to make eye contact with the pirate, but it was like looking at the stars above, and so she could not see his eyes well unless she looked a bit away from him.

"So, you're sorry for what you did?" she asked.

"Aye," said Longshanks. "But there be no repaying the debt; so on we march, ne'er to be free again, nor to see the light of day, nor feel the softness of love, nor the feel of the wind curving us down the cape…"

Jeddy shuffled her feet in and out of the sand beneath them.

"If I come back here next year, at this exact same time, will you be here?"

"Aye," said the pirate. "Doomed forever, we will be back."

"Does anyone ever see you?" she asked.

"Nay, lass, none but you," he answered.

"Why?"

The pirate's pale, shifting eyes looked up toward the sky.

"Maybe, lass, I sensed ye had a knowing mind, and could tell stories, and remember. Can ye do that, lass? Can ye remember us? Can ye remember me?"

"I can remember you!" said Jeddy, emphatic.

She could see his outline nodding.

"Then on we'll go," said Longshanks. "And maybe, lass, you'll be here again, and see us again, and maybe not. But the wind blows off the cape, and the storm draws nigh, and a young lass needs her sleep. Off with ye, and be a good lass, and do good things."

"I will," said Jeddy, and then the pirate and his line of shadowy men with their glimmering torches walked on, never leaving any tracks with their feet. Jeddy watched them walk beyond the darkened bathroom, and then they vanished. All the lights of the campground came back on. The owl lights glimmered at her, and she could swear one of them winked.

The door to the camper opened. Grandma whispered, "Get in here, girl! Storm's a comin' soon, and who knows what else."

Jeddy took a deep breath. She wanted to say in a rush everything that she had seen. But she stopped, and looked down the way, and no pirates marched with pale torches. But Grandma followed her eyes, and watched her mouth stretch into a thin line.

"We'll be back next year," Grandma told her.

Jeddy sighed and nodded. "Good," she said. "I want to come back every year." Grandma smiled at Jeddy, and led her inside, where she yawned and stretched out over the table bed.

Grandma looked once more outside, thinking back to days long buried under sand, and of ten pale lights bobbing up from the sea ahead of a gale, years ago. "They'll come back too," she whispered. She shut the camper door.

OTHER FUTURES
TALES OF THE GALAXY AND A PLACE CALLED EARTH

A HARD LANDING

The rocks pelted down around Kace, staccato little explosions in the speakers of her helmet. She slipped and slid, her eyes stinging from sweat. *This is a hot world,* she thought. Below her spread forth a mottled grey-brown valley. Far beyond, dun-colored hills bordered a dark blue, jagged mountain range.

She scanned the valley with her helmet lenses: nothing. No sign of the other ship. She glanced over her shoulder at the smoldering wreck behind her.

Well now. I'm in a situation.

Kace had tried contacting the other ship already. Static crinkled in her ears each time. The controls had flickered after her hard landing and shut off entirely. That wasn't supposed to happen, she knew.

Still in a daze, she took long, careful steps into the gravel of the hillside. Her boots hissed down in the loose dirt, exposing red soil beneath. It reminded her of the huge sand dunes near the lake back on Earth. She was glad to be going down, and not up, at least for now.

Plenty of time to go get supplies later. Maybe, she thought.

There were three large boulders down to her left, and not seeing any other shade so close by, she skidded down to them. She stumbled near the end and fell on her side. But soon she clambered up and made her way into the crevices of the boulders. She sank with relief into the shade, glad to be away from the ferocity of the binary suns above.

She felt the surge of coolness inside her helmet as the suit recycled her sweat. She leaned against the cool surface of one of the boulders. She felt just enough relief that she almost dozed off. Until she saw it.

On the side of the rock to her left, a long horizontal gash appeared. And inside it a dull orange something flickered. She pressed up against the rock behind her in shock. Then a small shift in the rock made her squeal, and she turned to look at it.

As with the other boulder, a slit glowed. Now there were two. Frantic, she stood, risking the hot sun again, and could see in the third boulder yet another opening. All three rocks were splitting in horizontal lines. And Kace could deny it no longer. She was looking at three huge eyes, and they were widening to look at her.

She staggered backward. The ground shook. She wheeled around to look at the valley. She could run for it maybe. Or she could run back to the ship and take her chances inside it.

The hillside rumbled and made her choice for her. A cascade of gravel tumbled down to her, and she fell onto her bottom and watched. Her ship was coming down to meet her.

Or rather, it was coming to the rocks. The rocks with her. That stared lidless and unblinking at her.

With her left hand she grabbed a gun from her utility belt and held it high. *SHHH-WAP!* The flare shot up.

Please see this. Please. Anyone.

Her ship slid down. She watched it warp and fold and buckle and pop, as something drew it under the shifting hillside. And then it disappeared.

But the eyes remained. And all she could do was wait, or run. Kace, under the heat of two stars, whose only relief had been the shade of boulders…which could eat a ship.

OVERDUE iN DEEP SPACE

Githiliad Library was not for the faint of heart, and most definitely not for the incurious mind. Its labyrinthine expanse burrowed into a roughly dumbbell-shaped asteroid, flung out far enough from its nearest star that nobody would ever think to seek it out if they didn't know about it. But if one held a membership there, they could find wonders beyond exploding stars and tourmaline-hued nebulae. So long as everything was turned in on time.

"Check out the latest psy-op and spy on yourself and other species! Borrow three minds for ten microseconds! Place a hold on the latest five thousand tomes from Birrian Bladesworth!" spoke the advertisements throughout the Eleven Systems of Quizond. These played on endless loops, broadcasting long after the Quizond sector had crumbled from relentless war. The dazzling little ads met marauders and pirates and looters, who came in for the last pickings of the once-grand civilization.

Those types no longer visited the library. The coded messages were treated as background noise, despite their persistence. The security system of the library had been breached long ago, and pirates pillaged whatever there had been of monetary value. With no one seeking value in knowledge or experience, the asteroid continued its slow, tumbling orbit, spinning out those lonely messages, never to be engaged again. Until Pozzan Delchar heard them.

Delchar was a cynical cyborg, often plugged into her ship, ever seeking more veencraft jewels for the mining guild. This freelance gig often took her through asteroid belts in various systems. Quizond's resources had attracted many miners over the ages, and various and sundry fuels and minerals had been extracted…leading to some of the very battles that left the sector a desiccated husk of a place. Worlds hung like empty nut shells, their skeletal societal remains pockmarked by treasure seekers.

But Delchar knew the odds were poor anyway, and she was tired. She kept replaying in her thoughts the final words from Zycadie, her partner for four months, who had gone in silent running ostensibly to escape the law. Delchar knew that Zycadie really was working on a new art piece for a high-paying Concatenation representative. This might have been something that Delchar could have applauded. But it meant their breakup. So those wounds were still fresh.

She skimmed the old asteroid mines, guiding her ship partly with her thoughts and partly with her hands. At times she was unsure which she could rely on more. The ship communed with her as well, and just now awoke from its slumber.

"Captain Delchar, there is a repeater broadcast," said the vessel, *Quell 5*, in a sleepy voice.

"You know how I feel about those things," said Delchar with a yawn.

"Yes," said *Quell 5*, "but as it's the Githiliad, I thought you might want to look for veencraft."

"The Githiliad?" Delchar rubbed her face with her half-metalloid hands.

"The library," answered *Quell 5*.

Delchar smirked. "And what might I want with a library? Do you really think there would be veencraft jewels there, *not* already taken ages ago?"

The ship considered. "Perhaps. I have access to its catalog, and it would seem you can, in fact, check out veencraft jewels."

Delchar laughed out loud. "What? Ridiculous."

"I can patch it through, and you can see for yourself," said the *Quell 5*, with a slight lilt to its normal droning voice.

"Fine," said Delchar, and then watched as her console screen flicked through various images of all the library's offerings. There appeared a page among the pictures dedicated to veencraft jewels. Delchar leaned back and squinted.

"Huh," she said. "How about that. But it's closed, yeah?"

Quell 5 answered, "It is still considered open."

"Really? After all this time, after war and everything?" Delchar was incredulous.

"It was deemed," *Quell 5* murmured, "that no library should ever close within the Quizond sector. No matter the circumstance."

"Surely there's nothing left—" Delchar began.

"I've checked," said the ship. "The jewels are there. You can go get them right now."

"Hmm," Delchar considered. "Well, you've certainly piqued my curiosity. All right, let's head there."

Quell 5 changed course and approached the lobular asteroid. Delchar allowed the ship to play its repeating message.

"It sounds like an absurd place, with that message," Delchar mused, and she steered the ship closer, noting various facets like giant green beads sticking out all along the asteroid's surface. These, she realized, were windows, or skylights of a sort. She discovered this shortly after docking.

There was a tussle at the docking bay, with Scampers peeling away old cables. Delchar shone a light on the helmeted creatures, and they zipped off, startled. They were harmless, and quite a cowardly people, only seeking others' junk.

"If there's anything left anywhere, those Scampers will take it, no matter how useless," said Delchar with disgust.

Quell 5 responded with a sort of hum, and then helped Delchar ease into docking position. She unhooked from her controls, rubbed the back of her neck where they had connected, and placed her helmet over her spiky indigo hair.

The helmet allowed the looping advertisement to continue, until Delchar silenced it. She slipped through an airlock door and found herself in a long hallway that lit up as she stepped along in the light gravity. There was some natural light, from the sun of that system, shining through those bead-like skylights. Delchar walked down the hall and reached an antechamber, and it lit up.

Dazzling green lights shone from the skylights, accompanied by a rising, glowing, golden light from an unknown source. Delchar then could see that, in all directions, shelves curved and twisted, and little winking lights rimmed each shelf. Some were purple, some were red. Delchar came to realize the red lights belonged to items that were checked out, and the purple items were available. Most of them were little cartridges of varying lengths. She pulled out one to examine it.

"Five ferries for Nebulat Crossing," she translated from the cartridge. "So," she said in this great, empty space, "I can check out…ferries. Well. I'll tuck that into my good-to-know file."

She paged *Quell 5*. "Where are the jewels?" she asked.

The ship responded in a sighing tone, as if just awakened, "Ask the librarian."

"There is no—" Delchar began. But she did see something. A little basket dropped down from the ceiling of the place, or perhaps it rose, depending on one's position. Within that basket huddled a small, six-branched creature, mostly made of circuits, and more of a cyborg than

Delchar herself. The basket opened and the creature looked out with four stalked eyes.

"Welcome to Githiliad!" it croaked. "I am Librarian. How can I help you today?"

Delchar wished she could rub her eyes; her helmet prevented her.

"I—I guess I'd like to…check out something?" she stammered.

"And what would you like? We have the latest mega-ships, mantle-cannons, orbiting party barges—"

"Um, veencraft jewels?" Delchar suggested.

Librarian curled its six branches inward, retracted its eyes, and made a huff. "Very well," and the basket shot off down a spiraling corridor. Delchar used her suit's thrusters to follow. As she flew past the shelves, music began playing. Notes like mournful teardrops plucked by unseen hands, or perhaps programmed by some intelligence, flooded through her helmet. And Delchar found herself appalled to be thinking of Zycadie.

"How did you have so little time for me?" she muttered.

Librarian halted.

"Oh, I didn't mean you," said Delchar, embarrassed.

Librarian opened its basket. "We have arrived."

It reached out with one of its appendages and used a sucker-print to open a clear case, wherein shone the opalescent veencraft jewels. And these weren't mere pebbles: they were large, larger than Delchar's hands.

"Wow!" she exclaimed. "And I can just…check these out?"

"Correct," said Librarian. "But only if you check one other item out."

"And…what's that?" Delchar asked, raising an eyebrow.

Librarian's basket-craft drifted up, so Delchar shot up a few shelves to join it. Librarian then plucked an object from a shelf, and its light turned red. The object was small and rectangular, and bits of thread extended from it in places.

"This," Librarian said grandly, "is a book."

Delchar laughed. "I know it's a book. I'm just…surprised to see one out here. I didn't think my people's objects were out here, especially something so old."

"Books never age," said Librarian in a flat tone. "Especially this kind."

Delchar shook her head. "What am I going to do with a book?"

"It is not merely a book," Librarian responded, all six branches of its body turning a bright purple. "It is said to endow the reader with great love, if given as a gift. The giver will receive that love in return."

Delchar shook her head. "I can check out ferry ships and highly valuable veencraft jewels. I can't imagine anyone I know wanting this."

"Not even Zycadie?" said Librarian.

Delchar flushed. "Hey! You're not supposed to read minds, it's the law!"

Librarian grew so purple it began to glow. "I do not read minds, but I do read ship manifests, for security reasons," it tutted. "And you've written the name Zycadie so many times that it created its own program on your ship, to the point it's invaded your dreams. Did you know that?"

Delchar stared. "I—no."

"Take the book to Zycadie," suggested Librarian. "What harm is there?"

"Look, Zycadie doesn't want to talk to me."

"Did Zycadie say that to you?" asked Librarian, its color beginning to dull.

"Um, well, no," admitted Delchar.

"Then take the book."

Delchar sighed, exasperated. "Can I get my crystals now?"

"Very well," said Librarian. "But remember. You are checking these items out, and they will be due far faster than you can imagine. Such is the way of things in a library."

"What—what happens if I don't get them back in time?" Delchar asked. For it had been her intention never to return those jewels, to say nothing of the book.

"Oh, you and your ship will be destroyed in due course," Librarian said nonchalantly.

Delchar snorted. "Sure," she said.

A soft crackling noise met her ears, and several bolts of purple lightning then converged all around Librarian. It grew out of its basket, into a pulsing, engorged, enormous creature, with its six stalks snapping in all directions.

Its voice boomed, "You will return your items before the due date."

Delchar sprang backward.

Librarian then shrank back into its small form. It sped over to the veencraft jewels, withdrew three, and returned to Delchar.

"Thank you for visiting Githiliad Library!" it chirped, and then it sped back up to its origin, beyond sight.

Delchar felt her suit trying to siphon off her nervous sweat to recycle it.

Quell 5 chimed in, "I think you should come back now."

Delchar wasted no time, although she did look longingly at all the shelves, and wondered what endless adventures one might have by checking something out at the library. She entered her ship, listened to its door hiss and the air equalize, and took off her helmet. She set the jewels securely into a bag, and then held the frazzled book in her hands.

"Hey, *Quell*," she said.

"Mmm?" mumbled the ship.

"Set a course for Myonlaat."

"But Zycadie said—" began the ship.

"Zycadie didn't actually say much," Delchar said. She swallowed and rubbed her face. "So I'm taking a chance."

"Setting course," said *Quell 5*. "But officially, I think it might be unwise."

Delchar nodded. "It might be. But I'm going to take my chances. It's been too long."

She held the book up.

"In fact, I'm overdue."

VOID MAGE

Gertie Hammond wandered down the railroad near her house, balancing upon slick silver track between red clay banks choked by kudzu. She was bored and she'd had a bad day. Time seemed stuck.

She rather disliked being fourteen and wanted to skip ahead to a time cliques didn't criticize her outfits, her face, or her family's lower income. Gertie chiefly wanted to write and draw, and she wanted a job that wasn't babysitting.

She trudged along the tracks, writhing from the crushing embarrassment of falling on her knees at school, bursting her pants. She'd begged to stay home the next day, but her parents refused. "Get back on the horse," they said. She preferred setting off on a heroic voyage, far from the shallow glints of teen queens' eyes.

She picked up one of the granite rocks that lined the track and hurled it down into a ravine toward an abandoned old tin roof, buckled and warped over decades. Its tremendous metallic crash satisfied her. She threw another, alternating hands. *TWONG*! That didn't dissuade her negative thoughts. It did, however, create a sonic disturbance that burst a fissure into the air above the track. And out of that fissure fell a person.

He righted himself and skidded briefly in the granite gravel. Gertie stared.

He was clad in raven-iridescent indigo, with long spikes of hair lightning white at the roots, and blue-black-purple at the ends. His outfit shimmered like living obsidian. Gertie felt as though a rock star had dropped before her.

"Ah, good, you're here," the person said, glancing toward her. The fissure in the air above him shimmered. "Come on, then. Before we're too late."

"What?" said Gertie, feeling stupid, but excited.

"Follow me. Ah, yes. Formalities." His stern brow softened. "I'm Delatken. Void Mage. And I need you to follow me, to save someone in the past, your future, and all that."

Gertie, staring with owl eyes, said, "I'm sorry?"

Delatken waved a fine-fingered hand and said, "No need for apologies. Unless you don't come, in which case, *then* you'll want to apologize to the people in the past and future you could have saved. Didn't you ask for this? I seem to recall your beseeching the Universe for some sort of purpose. A job, yes? Well, guess what? You've got it, but only if we leave right now. You *are* Gertie Hammond, yes?"

"Yes," Gertie managed to say.

Delatken nodded and bowed. "Nice to meet you officially. Let's jump into the sky."

Gertie looked over her shoulder, at shining tracks bending homeward, where she would dread school. She marched up to Delatken, noticing he smelled of something burning, but not unpleasant. She extended her hands and said, "I hope I can trust you."

"I wouldn't be here if you couldn't," said Delatken.

Seizing her hands, he lifted her like a balloon, and they rose together into the shimmering rift above their heads. Gertie fainted.

She woke briefly, tongue lolling, as Delatken marched with her in his arms through swirls of violet and magenta nothingness, dotted with forks of blue lightning.

"Where are we?" she asked thickly.

"Away from your mundane life."

With a whistling sound that rose to a high pitch until silent to her human ears, the lights and swirls went away. She stood with Delatken in a tower, glinting with violet-hued, diamond-paned windows. It felt like standing inside an amethyst.

"What is this place?" Gertie asked.

Delatken said, "This my watchtower, from which you can see everything. Past, present, future...although the latter is amorphous. It melts as quickly as you encounter it."

"Like cotton candy," mused Gertie.

Delatken laughed. "Like cotton candy."

"Why did you bring me here?" she asked. "I'm a nobody."

"You're anything but a nobody, Gertie Hammonds," said the mage. "You might help anyone, anywhere."

"From here?" she asked.

"From here," he said. He raised his arms. The violet diamond-shaped facets of the tower turned open. She could see through to different places and eras, some beautiful, some terrible. "It's all a little tiring for me lately. You've got a malleable imagination. I think it's just right for you."

Gertie swallowed. "I actually have to go home for dinner," she said reluctantly.

Delatken laughed and pointed to one of the diamonds. Gertie could see her mother setting the table and looking irritated.

"She's probably wondering why I'm not helping," said Gertie, wincing.

Delatken said, "Well, then, I'll take you back."

"But I can come back here?" she asked, torn.

He smirked and gestured around them. "Here, there, and anywhere. But for now, home."

He took her hand. She glanced at the brilliant sparkles of the tower's interior, realizing for a moment it resembled a lighthouse, but he pulled her back into the void-space of swirling color.

She found herself standing on the railroad. Delatken stood beside her.

"Well?" he said. "Throw the rock. Just the right frequency again, please. I don't want to end up with two heads or something!"

She stared and he laughed. "Farewell until…tomorrow?"

"I…yes," Gertie stammered. "Tomorrow."

"Until then, Gertie Hammonds. I think you've got a brilliant future ahead of you. To cotton candy!"

So she reached down, grabbed a stone, and threw it. Her aim was true. The metallic twang made her shudder. Delatken's image wavered, and with a small *crack*, he vanished. Gertie blinked, wondering if she had hallucinated everything. She walked slowly toward home until she heard her mother calling her name. Then she sprinted.

Inside her home, Gertie panted.

"What took you so long?" asked her mother, exasperated.

"I…got a job," Gertie said, beaming.

"A…what? What kind of job?"

Gertie heaped food onto her plate and watched its steam rise in a little puff that looked suspiciously purple.

"Making cotton candy," she said impishly.

Her mother shook her head. "Is this one of your tales, Gertie? When do you start?"

"Yesterday, today, and tomorrow, I think," said Gertie.

Her mother laughed.

"As long as you're home in time for dinner!"

THE SCAFFOLD

A spectacular crash of glass blasted through the hallway of the first floor of the Hansen Biology Building. Gale Thompson spilled her LB solution onto her lab coat, and it seeped onto her shoes. She scowled over its fetid reek, even as she trembled from the shock of the crashing glass. She craned her neck to see if Will had heard it, but he sat with headphones on, analyzing data on the lab computer. She sighed, set the solution down, and stepped out into the hall.

The hallway floor outside lab room 175 glistened with a pile of shattered glass. A tall man with dark, curly hair and stylish glasses emerged from the room, whistling, and walked with jaunty purpose all around the mess. Gale could see he brandished a shop broom like a rock star might hold a microphone at a concert. He swept and whistled, swept and whistled, his whistles and the clinking of glass echoing down the hallway from where she peered around the corner of her lab's door. It was late, 6:47 according to her phone, and 6:49 according to the fast analog clock wheeling its benign wand in a drab and economical circle perched on the wall opposite the door in the lab. Dr. Franks had left at 5:25 to go home; the grad students would drift in and out like the tide, but she, the lab tech, tended to stay late on Thursdays. She had little else to do except go home to feed her birds and watch TV.

She stared at the mess and dithered over what to do. But the man saw her, and she jerked instinctively but did not reenter the lab.

He laughed. "It's all right," he called. "Just cleaning up my mess."

Gale emerged fully and tugged at her light brown ponytail. "Are—are you all right?"

He was whistling again as he shoved the quite spectacular pile of broken glass of all sizes into one position.

"Feeling great!" he said. "Are you the new tech of Franks?"

Gale nodded. She stood awkwardly in the hall. She decided to walk toward him.

"Yeah. I'm Gale. Do you need help?"

The man set the broom against the wall and approached her. He wore fine Italian boots, she noted, had artfully distressed jeans, a fancy belt buckle, and a crisp, dark brown shirt. His eyes were hazel, and he was indeed quite tall as he looked down at her.

"I might! I'm Jack. Jack Cordeiro." He extended his hand for her to shake.

She blushed. "Oh! Dr. Cordeiro! I'm sorry. I didn't know you were back."

"Please," he said. "Call me Jack. Come in, if you have a moment?"

Gale could tell he caught a whiff of the spilled LB on her lab coat. Embarrassed, she quickly dashed back to her lab, doffed the coat, and returned. She followed Jack into Room 175. She found a chaotic scene inside, with piles of plastic zip bags spread out across the black lab benches. No one else was in the lab; the PI, Dr. Sykes, had taken the day off after receiving some bad news (so she had heard from Dr. Franks).

Jack gestured to a lab stool.

"As you can see," he said, "I have a bit of a mess on my hands. I need to get some of these in the deep freezer, but I'm not quite in the mental state to do that right now."

He looked cheerful enough, Gale thought, and even kind of elated as he smiled. But the glassware in the hall…

"I nearly dumped them all on the side of the road," he confessed, grinning at her.

She could feel the little "11" forming in her forehead as she considered that statement. He laughed.

"I know. Crazy, right?" And he hummed. He sorted through some of the plastic bags, which had been labeled hastily with black marker. "I'm not as interested in the plants though. I'm interested in something that came back from the desert."

"The desert?" Gale echoed.

"Yes. Atacama."

"Oh, yes, the group went down last summer, and they've just gone back, right?" she asked.

"Yes," said Jack. "Only we've not heard from them in a few days. They did send some samples back, which, remarkably, made it through customs."

"Samples of what?" asked Gale, for she knew that the plants before her did not grow in any desert. They were, if she had to guess, from some kind of deciduous tree. Maybe beech.

Jack walked around to the back of the lab and extravagantly waved his arm for her to follow. She did. There were Petri dishes laid out in an orderly fashion, carefully labeled in a different handwriting from Jack's, with what looked like coordinates on them. Inside each dish were what looked like sand, and soil, and some mix thereof. Different dishes held slightly different looking samples.

"Soil's not my purview," Jack told her. "These were supposedly full of seeds, but those have been sifted out. I don't know who these samples are for. I *do* know that I don't quite like them. Watch this."

He retrieved a hulking Geiger counter from the opposite bench and turned it on. He waved it over the dishes, and the machine buzzed and crackled. Gale backed away.

"How dangerous is it?" she asked.

"Not so much now," smirked Jack. "But whenever the meteor hit, I guarantee the animals at the time didn't think so."

"How long ago?" Gale wondered.

"Long," said Jack. He adjusted his high-end glasses. Then he looked over them at her.

"But that's not the most interesting thing about these. And I think, Gale, I might be losing my mind."

With that extraordinary proclamation, Jack waved his arm and said, "Look what happens when I approach them up close."

She watched as he walked up to the dishes and held a hand close to them. The grains inside rose toward his hand.

"What?" said Gale, breathless. "Why are they doing that?"

"No idea," answered Jack. "I wouldn't ask you to do the same, but—"

She surged forward and held her hand over the dishes and the grains leaped up, and the dishes burst open and spilled their contents all over the lab floor. She and Jack jumped back and then found themselves creeping backward toward the lab door. For the dirt began arranging itself in ornate patterns on the floor, and making little bridges from the floor into the air, like so much scaffolding, made of sand and dirt from a moment of impact by a large object into the earth eons ago. The connections bridged and stretched and bridged again until something resembling a possible creature emerged. The scaffolding stepped forward, purposefully, toward Gale and Jack.

"My God," whispered Jack. "What did they bring back from that desert? And what happened to everyone who's there now?"

Gale swallowed. "I don't know. But I think we should *run!*"

RODER

I am in love with a machine.

Roan blinked. It just came to her, this thought, this dance of neurons firing and receptors bathing in torrents of dopamine. She looked down at her hands, once delicate and lovely, now careworn and shriveling around the knuckles. The hands of someone who worked hard cleaning, holding children against her breasts, chopping vegetables, pulling watercolor across paper, writing…the hands of a human who loved a machine.

So, how did that happen? She could imagine someone else asking this, but really she asked it of herself as well. What part of the history of this made any sense?

I tried to figure out how this machine worked, and I ended up falling in love with it. It didn't seem like a very convincing answer. But for some time, it was all she could come up with.

She did not remember much before the day she had met him. It was warm sun on frozen ground; it was a great crack in a deep lake of ice, the exchange and the recognition in his eyes. A machine's eyes. And yet she knew them.

And many had pontificated on whether or not a machine had a soul. But she knew this one did, only after meeting his eyes. And that began her strange journey to now.

She thought back to that sweltering day.

She rocked back and forth in the passenger seat of an ancient pickup over a farm road with deep ruts. The truck was unconverted: that is, it still took alcohol. The fact it worked at all, or that the farmer could patch the tires to keep it rolling, amazed Roan.

Mr. Fitzgibbons looked askance at her with his rheumy-pale eyes. Furrows and folds undulated across his ancient, sunburned face.

"Whatchu want with that thang, anyway?" he had asked her before she had climbed aboard.

"I'm here," and Roan cleared her throat before continuing, "because the Sheldonian heard about an Outlier. I'm on the beat right now, because

Trina is on maternity leave." She wiped her sweating brow. Streaks of lank brown hair irritated her cheeks.

"Well hit don't work no more, just so's you know," Mr. Fitzgibbons said, shrugging.

Roan chewed the inside of her right cheek, twisting her mouth as she did so.

"I know. None of them work anymore. But I've never actually *seen* one," she replied.

The truck hit a deep valley of grass and drying mud and sent her flying upward out of her seat. Her teeth clamped down on her tongue and she yelped.

"You coulda been dropped in," the farmer said to her, clucking his non-bitten tongue.

I coulda been a lot of things, she wanted to shout at the old fellow.

"I appreciate the ride, just the same," she answered flatly.

She sighed. She hoped this wasn't a dead end…although it quite literally was, for the truck pulled up to an overgrown and faded red barn. Just barely, on its tin roof, she could read "SEE ROCK CITY" in great letters. *Where was Rock City?* she wondered. *Why would I want to see it?*

She pushed the door open with a horrible screech. She slid out, and her messenger bag fell to the ground among tall Queen Anne's lace flowers. The farmer leaned over to watch her and squinted.

"Hit's in the back, with the other tools. You want me to stick around?"

Roan shouldered her bag and sighed.

"No," she said. "No, thank you. I'll call for you." But really she thought it might be worth the walk back, despite the heat.

Mr. Fitzgibbons nodded and put the truck in reverse. She watched him pull around, skid a bit, and send up some small puffs of dirt. Then the truck pivoted and pitched and rollicked back along the weedy road, back to the old man's home.

She turned back to the barn. Adjusting her bag, she waded through tall grass, wild chicory, more Queen Anne's lace, and panicking grasshoppers. The door stood ajar, and its opening was laced with cobwebs. She looked around for a stick, and then brandished it to sweep away the webs. She pressed her utility necklace to cast light into the dark barn. It stank of animal droppings.

The ceiling rose high above her, with a hayloft and various farm equipment and old hoses hanging here and there. It looked like some great, disemboweled, rotting creature whose carcass she explored. She pushed through more webs and stepped over the dirt floor. She found the tools and sneezed. And in the cloud of droplets from her sneeze, a small shard of sunlight from outside shone through and suspended them. And on the other side of this tiny cloud, she could see eyes.

"Hup!" she yelped, and she stumbled backward. The eyes glowed as green rings, and they adjusted. Then they shut off.

What? was all she could think.

She leaned toward the figure, and saw the outline of a humanoid shape, partially obscured by shadow and a thick layer of ochre-colored dust. The eyes were switched off, and dark. She stepped closer, and found herself staring up at this tall figure, with its smooth face, with no sharp angles. She reached out and touched that face…

The eyes flashed open, and two hands seized hers.

"Ah!" she cried, and she snatched her hand away. The being let her go easily.

Its green eyes shone and swiveled, and it turned its head down to her. It opened its mouth, and a deep wheeze came out. Then a metallic sound left its throat, for all the world like a cough echoing in a tin can.

"Ha-ha-ha-ha-HELLO!" the metallic voice said, and to her it sounded male. The robot stood still and held out its hands, where it had released hers gently.

Roan stared in open-mouthed surprise. "Hello!" she responded, not wanting to be rude. Then she thought about how absurd that thought was, and she laughed. And then she sneezed. Another cloud of droplets.

The being watched the vapor dissipate. Roan blushed.

"Sorry," she said.

"Ble-ble-ble-ble-BLESS. YOU!" said the robot.

She giggled. "Thank you."

"Wa-wa-wa-wa-WHAT is your NAME?" it asked her, and politely, it held out a hand. She found herself taking it this time. It was soft, and large, and she could have fit both her small hands into it. It squeezed her hand so carefully that she felt her mouth twitch at the corner in amusement.

"I'm Roan Beverly," she replied, grinning, looking up. "You're so *tall*," she said, and then she blushed again. "Sorry, just…just noticing. Um. What's your name?"

"Ma-ma-ma-ma-MY name is RODER," said the android. And with much creaking and squeaking, Roder shook where it stood, sending dust everywhere.

"Nice to meet you, Roder," said Roan. "I didn't know if you were still operational. Mr. Fitzgibbons said you might be."

"I-I-I- am very STIFF," said Roder. It listed a bit, and Roan reached out to grab it.

"Caught you!" she said, holding onto Roder. Roder's eyes spun and glowed more brightly.

"Tha-Tha-Tha-Tha-THANK you, Roan Beverly," said Roder, still holding her hands.

"You're welcome," she answered, "but please, call me Roan."

"Ro-Ro-Ro-ROAN it is then," responded Roder.

Roan laughed. "You're not what I expected you to be at all."

A deep sort of whine emerged from its throat.

"I'm sorry, I didn't mean to offend you," she said.

"You-You-YOU could NOT, Roan," replied Roder. "Will-you help-me-walk?"

"Yes," Roan replied, and she held onto his arm, and watched Roder work its legs and step tentatively forward.

"I-I-I-must WORK," said Roder, and Roan smirked.

His voice is loosening up. And then she thought, *Is he a* he?

"Roder," she said quietly, "are you gendered?"

Roder's green irises phosphoresced. "I-I can be," came the reply. "Would-you-like-for-me-to-be?"

And Roan was amazed at such a statement. "I...I hadn't really thought about it. I kind of thought you were male because of your deeper voice, but didn't want to assume."

"I-I can-be-male," said Roder.

"If you want," said Roan, "but it's *your* preference."

"To-To-TODAY I will be male then," replied Roder.

"Very well," said Roan. "It really isn't up to me: it is your own truth."

"You-YOU are-FEMALE," said Roder.

"Yes," agreed Roan. "I do identify as female."

Roder seemed to study her.

"Are-ARE you-a-mother?" he asked softly.

Roan erupted in laughter. "No," she replied.

"You-YOU like-to-laugh," noted Roder.

Roan considered. "I suppose so. I haven't laughed so much in a while though. I had...maybe forgotten how."

"I-I-I like the sound-of-your-laughter," Roder told her.

Roan still held Roder's hands, and they grew warm to the touch. She dusted off his shoulders. "There," she said, "good as new, or nearly."

"I-I am-OLD," replied Roder.

"Well," said Roan, "you don't look so old to me. You look as though you've been...suspended for some time. But you are well preserved."

Roan helped him walk out of the barn. He strode stiffly, his knees barely bending, and she could not help but think of *The Wizard of Oz* and the Tin Woodman. Roder did not have visible joints, and she had no oil can. But she remembered that Dorothy helped the Tin Woodman until he could walk by himself. So that was what Roan would do.

This proved to be somewhat more of a challenge for Roder than Roan anticipated. The problem with the dirt road became apparent quickly. Roder could not bend his knees fully enough to cope with the ruts in the road, and so sometimes he tumbled into them. Roan pulled him back up again.

"Th-th-THANK you," said Roder. Roan stifled her laughter.

So it was a long time back, nearly an hour, to Mr. Fitzgibbons' house. There it stood, its red-painted roof now faded and rusted, its gables sagging, and its trim grey. The porch bowed, and a lone hog snored there, asleep. His truck was parked off under a great oak tree, and that was where he kept a shed with mosquito netting windows. Roan and Roder, now more loosened up, approached the shed.

Roan could see the old farmer's feet propped up on the windowsill. Like the hog on his porch, he had fallen asleep. Roan hesitated, but then tapped lightly on the screen door to the shed.

A long snort erupted from the man, and he scratched himself and his legs dropped down. He coughed for such a long time that Roan worried he might collapse. Roder moved forward into the shed.

"Mi-Mi-MISTER Fitz-gibbons," he said, and the old fellow jumped and stopped coughing.

Mr. Fitzgibbons took off his faded engineer cap and slapped his legs with it.

"RODER!" he bellowed. "I'll be damned!" He turned his watery-pale eyes to Roan and said, "You got hit tuh work again!"

Roan felt her cheeks burn. "He is working again," she answered evenly.

She watched the farmer look at his watch and make a little swipe on its surface, as if he were wiping something off its face. Then Mr. Fitzgibbons stretched his back, and walked around Roder, who watched him with his steadfast green gaze.

"They'll be glad," said the farmer. "Not too many of these work anymore, and really they were the best ones."

Roan worried over this remark. But she kept watching as he inspected the android.

He took a rag and wiped off a part of Roder's lower back. His whole body looked as though it were clothed, even though he did not wear clothing. So the part of his back the farmer wiped would have been between his waist and his ribs, if he had any. And Roan could then see some faint letters: Sheldon Model 5He7Sp.1.8.4 – ROTOR.

ROTOR.

"That's why you call him…Roder?" she asked the farmer.

He nodded. "Says it right there: RODER."

Roan's lips twitched.

She walked around to face Roder. He stared at her face.

"You-you-YOU want to laugh," he said seriously.

"N-no," stammered Roan, embarrassed and a little ashamed.

She looked away from him, but his arms reached out and lightly took hold of her shoulders. She stared up at him.

The farmer kicked Roder in the backs of his knees, and he fell to the ground. Roan cried out.

"Why'd you kick him?" she yelled, and she bent to help Roder up.

"That thang shouldn't touch you," said Mr. Fitzgibbons, with a wild look in his eyes.

"He didn't hurt me," snapped Roan.

"Hit won't hurt you," said the farmer. "They're on their way. They'll shut hit down, and take hit in for recycling."

Roan went cold.

"What do you mean?" she asked, shaking.

"The Sheldon folks are on their way," the old man said simply, and he exited the shed and squinted up at the sky. Roan followed, pulling Roder along. "There they are right now."

Roan froze.

A craft descended, down-drafting and sending the oak tree's canopy swaying. And on this side of this matte-blue craft, she could see the glossy insignia of Sheldon Cybernetic Solutions, a concave triangle.

For a few seconds, Roan contemplated seizing Roder, jumping in the old pickup truck, and driving off. Of course nothing about that would go well, as she did not have

the keys, did not know how to drive it, and would be apprehended very soon. She would come to regret not trying though.

A pilot remained on board, and a technician exited the skycraft. He was lean and of medium height, with a clear visor over his face. His hair was sandy blonde, and his eyes were dull grey. His outfit, dark blue and with the Sheldon emblem on its shirt pocket, held all manner of pouches and tool compartments.

"Hit grabbed ahold of her," announced Mr. Fitzgibbons. "Didn't know hit still worked, or I'd have called in sooner."

The technician turned to Roan and asked, "Are you all right, ma'am?"

"I'm *fine*," said Roan with force. "He didn't hurt me at all."

The technician approached Roder, who stared passively down at him, and then pulled out a small wand that looked like a screwdriver. The tech turned it on, and it emitted a light and a small pop. He drew this wand straight down the front of Roder, and Roan knew then it was a laser. Roder's front flapped open, his innards revealed.

Roan screamed.

Roder stared at her.

"Ro-Ro-ROAN," he said. "You-can see-inside-me."

And Roan leaned over and vomited.

"What are you doing to him?" she cried.

The tech, unfazed by her reaction, looked over his shoulder and said, "Shutting it down. Glad it's still operational; they'll want to use the parts in Archive Division. Now it won't hurt anyone."

"HE DIDN'T HURT ME OR ANYONE ELSE!" screamed Roan.

Roder said quietly, "Ro-ROAN, it-is-okay. I-will not-feel-it."

Roan's face swelled from tears. She choked and said, "Please don't do this. Please don't take him."

The tech tilted his head and stared at her. "Ma'am, this thing is a tool, you know that, right? It's a ROTOR unit. It's not a person. Now if you'll excuse me, I need to get it on board. Mr. Fitzgibbons, thank you for bringing it to our attention. We'll take it from here."

Roan ran at Roder and threw her arms around him, despite his open front and the various exposed circuitry.

"Roder," she said, her voice shattered, "I'll come and look for you. I promise."

"ROAN," he said simply. And she kissed his cheek.

He raised his hand to that cheek.

The technician shoved himself in between them. The tech pressed something with his wand, and Roder's head lolled over, and his eyes went dim.

Roan let out a wail. She watched helplessly as the tech hoisted Roder onto a hand truck and wheeled him onto the little ship. And up it shot into the hazy summer sky, taking Roder away.

She held her promise. She lodged her official complaints, and then she shook off her anguish and set to work. Every night she worked to try to find where Roder had been taken. She surmised that a recycling facility would be in a more urban area, and so she researched any that she could find having to do with robotics. After several days, she found nothing, and she sat in her apartment one evening, checking in with various contacts that might be able to help. One of them knew a technician who repaired Sheldon robotics.

She spoke to him as the late afternoon sun sliced a golden wedge into her living room from the window.

"I'm looking for a Sheldon Model, a Roder—I mean, a Rotor model," she said to the man, whose glint-specs concealed his eyes slightly with their constant panels and words that only he could make out.

"What's the number?" he had asked, clearly bored, and distracted by the media in his glint-specs. She told him the number. He sighed, which irritated her. "Oh. Yeah, we don't make those anymore. Sorry."

"Wait!" she cried, twitching her hair over her shoulder. "Can't you just tell me…if, say, you had a broken model and wanted it fixed, or"— and she hated to say it—"recycled, where would it be taken?"

The man took a breath and puffed it out in a whistle. "I don't know why anyone would want to repair those, since there are better models for cheaper."

Roan's heart sank.

"But as for recycling? I'd try CytWerks over in Tuxton."

Roan bit her lip. "Thank you," she said, and she grabbed her keys and left her apartment.

She hailed a car. Her driver was appreciative. "I get so few customers who appreciate a *real* driver," the man said.

Roan winced. *How do you know what is real?* But she was in no mood to debate him. She had one singular goal: find Roder.

She stepped out of the car at the edge of an old factory, which snorted and grunted and belched out material she was quite sure was not up to code. The car would go no farther. She walked along a gravel-scattered, cracked pavement truck road around the perimeter of the factory. She could see no one, but the sounds disturbed her.

"Awf-awf-awf!" a very humanlike voice shouted, echoing in the twilight. "I work! I work!" and then some gurgling sounds poured forth before the voice clipped short.

Jesus, she thought, shuddering. It took twenty minutes to walk around the outside of the fence. She hoped to find a way in. She knew eventually there would be an official entrance. But the only thing she found was a gate leading to a container dock. She could see there had been a truck recently, by the tracks in dried mud from yesterday's rain. She approached the gate.

Another voice ricocheted into the darkness. "BAR-er, BAR-er, BAR-er!" it yelled in a high pitch, not unlike a child's. Roan covered her mouth in horror. "Let me go! BAR-er! BAR-er!" And then a crackling sound, and then silence.

"What are they doing to them?" she whispered.

She could stand it no longer. She would climb the fence. At first she hesitated, wondering if it would shock her. She found that it did not. This was a barebones operation, a place of destruction, of breaking down, of ending. It was a place that nobody cared about what happened, because to the outside world, everything entering it was considered trash. Her hands sweated and she clawed her way awkwardly up and over the fence.

Surely they did not bring Roder here, she felt herself hope. But somehow she knew, deep down, that her gentle friend must be inside. It propelled her to try to find him. She slipped through a dank, overheated hallway to the left of the dock. It was dark and glowed deep red, and throbbed, and she felt as though she had entered the mouth of something with insatiable hunger. More screams and shouts and broken, mechanical voices.

Roan's innards convulsed. She stole around, seeing the backs of apparent humans in the distance. Finally she came upon a vast room, full of tracks in the ceiling, and chains, and belching equipment that pounded and scraped and steamed. Sparks flew here and there as the limbs of various robots were plucked apart.

They're sentient, and they're being destroyed.

Roan wanted to scream. The equipment noise was deafening, but it was not loud enough to cover the agonized voices of the artificial people being dismantled. She noted that the human workers wore earplugs, so they could not hear the equipment…or the suffering.

She dared to flit here and there while backs were turned, and ultimately found what she had come for, an area piled with robot bodies, some of whom moved a bit, or groaned. They were caged in on all sides and could not leave. She searched and searched for Roder. She could not see him. And this left her with relief, but also despair for the other robots.

I will shut this place down. I will tell everyone what I have found here, and I will end this. And she clenched her teeth. She lowered her head and decided to leave.

But then a voice made its way out of the cage. "R-Roan," it said. Roan jerked, and ran to the cage. A shuffling and shifting parted various robots, as they let someone through. And it was Roder, and his eyes glowed at the site of her, but he was bent over and still ruined from his capture.

"ROAN," said Roder, more loudly, and she held her finger to his lips. She reached through the cage, and he did as well, and their hands intertwined.

"You-you came for me?" Roder asked. Roan trembled.

"Yes," she answered. "Of course I did, oh, Roder," and she wept.

"Do-do not cry," said Roder softly. "It will not last long."

"No," said Roan. "I have to get you out of here. I don't want you to…to be…recycled. Roder, they're killing your kind."

Roder reached as far as he could through the cage, and Roan reciprocated, and they held each other.

"They-they won't stop," said Roder.

"I will stop them!" Roan said firmly. Roder tried to reach her cheek, where tears shone in the dim light.

"You-you are so kind, Roan," said Roder. "I did not know I could feel so warm."

Roan laughed gently through her tears.

"There-there is your laugh," said Roder, almost melodically.

Then something prodded her sharply from behind.

"What are you doing here?" a voice bellowed loudly. Roan whipped around to see three workers staring at her, their ears covered, their faces and jumpsuits smeared with grease and grime.

One worker spoke to something on his wrist.

"We've called security," said the first man. "Nobody is allowed in here. Now get out!"

"I can't!" cried Roan. "My friend is in here. Please let him out!"

"Ma'am, these are machines to be recycled," said the man.

"He's not a machine!" Roan shouted. "He's a person! He cares about me, and I care about him!" And she and Roder held hands through the fence.

The man looked from Roan to her hands to Roder, and back to Roan. He looked over his shoulder at the other man, who had called security.

"Page Nielsen," he told him. "We've got a true one."

The man proceeded to open the cage, with the other men standing guard behind in case any of the robots tried to escape. The ones with eyes all stared. The man then entered the cage, and heavily walked to Roder, and seized him, and dragged him out, bent over, his innards flickering.

"You're hurting him!" exclaimed Roan. She rushed at Roder, her alarm giving her the strength to push the large man out of the way, and she and Roder knelt on the floor, lit from the sparks of another robot being butchered above them.

"You're free, you're free," gasped Roan, and Roder reached up and held her face in his hands.

"YOU-you saved me," Roder said. And they embraced for several minutes, while Roan fussed with his damaged parts and reassured him.

"I'll get you out of here," she said.

Then she felt firm hands on her shoulders. She turned to look up at a slender man and an athletic-looking woman, both sleek in long grey lab coats.

"We'll take it from here, ma'am," the woman said to Roan.

"What do you mean? I'm taking him with me," Roan protested.

"Sorry, ma'am, he is a true one, so we will need to remove him from this property and return him to Sheldon for repair and study," said the woman.

"Come with me," the slim man said to Roder, and he pulled the robot up. He scanned Roder with a little wand and nodded.

"He's good to go," the man said to the woman.

"No," Roan said. "NO! He's coming with *me!*"

The woman turned to the factory workers, and said dismissively, "Security is ready to come in. I apologize for the disruption. Have a good night, gentlemen."

And she and the other Sheldon worker held Roder's arms between them.

"No!" cried Roan, and she ran forward and seized Roder's waist from behind. "Please, please don't take him. He's a person, he cares, and I am his friend. I will take care of him, I promise."

"He's not your property, ma'am," the woman said crisply. "I suggest you make a quick exit before they press charges."

"Roder!" cried Roan, and Roder stopped firmly and would not budge. She crashed into him and held him tightly in her arms, and he strained against his injuries and clasped her close, pressing her face against his neck.

"D-dear Roan," he said.

"Oh, Roder, I will stop them, I will," she said breathlessly. "I will find you again."

"I-I know you will try," said Roder. "R-Roan," and at that moment a security guard entered the factory and seized Roan.

"Do-do not hurt Roan," said Roder to the Sheldon workers and to the guard. "She-she-she is dear to me."

Roan cried out as the guard separated them, and Roder was taken away, she knew not where. "Roder, Roder!" she called to him. "I will find you, I will take care of you! I promise!"

She tried her best, but all her contacts shrugged her off, or warned her against looking further. A "true one" meant that Roder had achieved true sentience, and wherever Sheldon had taken him, they were not willing to relinquish such a valuable asset. Roan did not stop looking.

"When are you going to let this GO?" said Samuel.

"I'm not," said Roan. "Stop suggesting that I do. I will still look."

"It's been TEN YEARS," said Samuel.

"It's been nine years and eight months and three days," said Roan.

Samuel shook his head. "The kids even—"

"Would you stop bringing them into this? It has nothing to do with the kids."

"They write COMICS about this thing, they draw PICTURES," protested Samuel.

"If you don't like it, just fucking leave, Samuel," Roan hissed. "I made a promise. I'm keeping it."

"What about the promise to ME?" said Samuel. "It's a goddamned machine, and I swear you give more of a shit about it than you do me."

"Then go," said Roan.

And Samuel did leave. Roan gasped in relief when he filed for divorce. There would be joint custody, but he had tried to take it, questioning Roan's sanity. The judge had tossed out such an accusation. She had even admonished Samuel: "She is an investigative reporter. She has worked on countless cases over the years, finding those who slipped through the cracks of the justice system. The fact you had such a problem with this one case is just that: your problem."

Roan stood in her kitchen one late summer evening. The kids were in bed. The windows were open, and she could hear katydids. She stared at her worn hands. She saw drops of water fall on them. Her tears.

Shiiiiifff, shiiiiifff. Roan jumped. Something was walking across the lawn, something slow, through the tall grass. Somewhere, a hound bayed, and its cacophonous barks sent shivers all through her. She readied a weapon.

Suddenly brilliant lights shone from above onto the lawn.

What? she thought.

"Look! Look!" came shouts. The boys!

"Hush!" she called up the stairs.

"No, Mom, look!"

And she turned her eyes, and found that the flashlight glow from her children's window illuminated a tall figure walking through the lawn, carefully, slowly. She wiped her greying hair from her face.

"How?" she asked the air, and she gasped.

Trembling, she ran to the door and turned on the porch light. She flung the door open.

"RODER!" she shouted, and there he stood, smudged and dragging parts, and his body gashed here and there. His damaged front sagged. Bits of the circuitry gleamed and fizzled in the night air.

But his eyes still shone green, and they stared at Roan.

"It's you!" Roan said softly. Roder approached her. *Can he speak?*

"Ro-ROAN," he said, and she wept then.

"How, how are you here?" she asked.

"So-so-SOMEONE saw your-your ARTICLE," he said to her. "And-and found-me in another abandoned-factory. I-do-not know his-name. He-fixed-me enough to WORK, and-he brought-me to YOUR-street."

"Oh my God," said Roan, shaking, and she laughed.

"Your-your LAUGHTER," said Roder. "I-remembered-it. Your-laughter brought me back."

Roan ran at him and seized him.

"You-YOU can-see all my-insides," Roder said, warning her. "I-am-OLD. And-BROKEN."

"Not to me, Roder," said Roan. "You're complete. I love you."

TOPAZ SUNDERED

She leaned over and vomited. Hands seized her hair, but too late: she felt fingers catch in her tangles.

"Ow," she protested, swallowing, sweating profusely.

"We need to get away from this thing, Vix," said Fran.

"I have to get more," protested Vix, not looking at Fran, and she approached the great stone before her.

It gleamed in rough facets of deep gold, bronze, brown, shot through with palest yellow like the first sunshine after a rain. Long shafts of light from high above danced within the crystal. It enraptured them, even pragmatic Fran. But the ore was known to sicken anyone who stayed around it for long.

"You're obsessed," hissed Fran. "We have enough. More than enough! Come on!"

"I just—just need a little more," Vix replied, gagging, holding her hands out to the crystalline stalagmite.

She struck it with a wrist-blade again, so that more of it shaved off. Her hands trembled now, and she could not catch the translucent golden shavings. She fell to her knees, swallowed again, and began shoving the pieces of crystal into her sampling pack.

Fran scrambled behind her. "God," she said, her voice low, "I don't know what's happening, but something is moving down the path behind us. *Hurry!*"

A puff of sickly yellow dust billowed into the chamber, and Vix knew, deep down, it was likely too late for them both. Fran seized her by the elbow and forcibly moved her back up the way they had come in. Their gossamer rope dangled from the opening of the cave above.

"Climb!" cried Fran, but Vix felt herself go sleepy. She looked at her hands, and they were covered in a soft, shimmery smear of gold flecks. Those tiny crystals swirled on the prints of her palms and fingers and absorbed into her skin.

She laughed in a little hiccupping voice and sagged to the floor of the cave.

Fran squeaked at her, and turned to see the dust filling the chamber, and growing. Something within it rumbled and flickered, like myriad eyes. She pulled on Vix, whose eyes lolled in her head, and her tongue spilled out of the corner of her mouth.

"Vix!" cried Fran, but Vix was lost to her for now. She strained and managed to lift Vix up and wrapped the rope around her. "I'll just have to carry you up," and Fran really believed that she could, for adrenaline pulsed through her to the point she thought she might glow.

But the dust had filled the chasm and obscured the light above. Its strange, inner light, flickering like tiny golden, winking eyes dazzled poor Fran. She tried to fight the urge to look at the great crystal, but she felt pulled toward it. She could look at the crystal, or this dust-being. She liked neither choice.

"Why do you fight?" a voice asked her, low and soft, and almost pleasant.

"P-please," Fran said, "we're going. We're sorry, just—just please let us go. We won't come back. We won't log the location. We're sorry we took—here, I'll dump it all out."

The smoke-dust surrounded her and Vix, whose eyes flitted back and forth as though she were spinning. Everything looked muted gold now, a soft wash of ochre, with the only light coming from the being speaking through the dust.

"You already stole what cannot be replaced," the calm voice said to Fran.

Fran shut her eyes to the thing, and would have covered her ears, but she wanted to hold onto Vix, no matter what happened. She strained to keep her eyes closed, but she could feel the approach of the being like warm breath all over her body, on her neck, against her eyelids. She could not control herself, and her eyes shot open.

Golden flames, thousands, millions, trillions beyond count, they all flickered in her vision, burrowed into her mind, and yet they all seemed to coalesce into an eye staring at her from across an unfathomable space. Fran could feel her sanity being flayed off her, and suddenly she realized what was happening. This thing made her feel what the great crystal felt. She threw her hands out and met something solid. Every sound muffled, and she screamed. She was trapped *inside* the great crystal. Vix remained outside of it, splayed on the ground of the cavern.

"Vix!" Fran cried, and she pounded on her topaz-hued prison from within. "VIX!"

Fran panicked the moment she realized she would run out of air inside this great gem. She could scarcely move around within it, and every part of her skin felt burned. She knew it would seep into her skin just as it had with Vix.

"Vix, please, please," she gasped, and then she knew she really did have to stop talking. But she pounded on her crystalline prison walls just the same.

The shapeless being began to coil above Vix's form and spin slowly. She twitched where she lay, and blinked, and moaned, and finally began to stir. Fran again pummeled the crystalline walls around her, but Vix could not hear her. She lifted her head and then let it fall again, for everything spun. She felt nauseous, and would have vomited again, but her stomach had spent itself. In her vertigo, she could not make out much around her, just the ochre-colored dust cloud and its flickering and swirling lights spinning above her.

"Fran," she said hoarsely, but she could not see the crystal, for the amorphous being blocked her view.

"Why did you take what is not yours to take?" a mellow voice asked, echoing in the cave.

"Huh?" Vix murmured. "I'm a miner. We're miners. Where—where's Fran?"

The being's flames swirled into an eye shape in front of her face. Vix snapped to attention then, and jerked backwards, her hands digging into the rocks beneath her. She could feel something wet, and knew she'd cut herself. Her backpack had also caught on the rocks and ripped. She frantically reached back and felt to see how large the hole was, and if any of her samples had fallen out. They hadn't.

"What do you want?" she asked. "Where's Fran?"

The shape, with its amber-gold-ochre-flame iridescence dizzying her, asked again, "Why do you take what is not yours?"

"I—we need it," Vix said, and her alertness rebounded. She turned her head slowly and could just see the tip of the great crystal, and a shape within it. She cried out and pushed herself up on her elbows. The smoke crept all around her.

"Let her go!" she screamed.

"We cannot do that," came the answer, and the large eye-shape turned toward the crystal. It withdrew its smoke and dust back within itself so that Vix could see the stone more clearly.

"No!" she cried. Fran had sunk to the ground, unconscious. "Get her out! Get her out! She can't breathe!"

With everything slow and painful, she found it difficult to stand, but she managed it, and she shuffled and stumbled toward the crystal.

"Fran," she croaked, her hands on the crystal. "Fran!"

Her friend did not respond.

Weeping, enraged, Vix shoved her vomit-sticky hair out of her face, and smeared the talc-soft crystal remnants off her hands onto her pants. She pounded on the stone while the creature began swirling all around her and the stone, and Fran within it.

"Why are you doing this?" Vix moaned. "Please let her go!"

"You have taken from us," the voice replied simply. "So shall we take from you."

Vix stared into the mass of flickering orange-gold-red lights in the eye of the creature.

"We needed the stone," she said hastily, "so we can live. We mine. We—we take ores and sell them for money, so we can live."

"You take a part of us that cannot be replaced," the creature said calmly.

"Please," Vix begged, "she's going to die in there. I'll give you all my samples. Just please let her go."

"Tell us," the voice said, placidly, as if observing sunny daffodils on a green lawn, "why do you think your lives matter more than ours?"

Vix was desperate. "We didn't know you were alive," she protested. "How could we have known?"

"You knew," said the voice. "Your sensory organs responded to us, and found us irresistible, and you kept coming back for more."

Vix shook with tears and pounded on the crystal's facets. "It's all my fault. I couldn't stop, she even warned me. It's not fair. Put me in there instead."

"No."

Vix wailed. "Why not? Fran is innocent!"

"You must serve penance for what you have done," said the voice, almost musical.

Vix cast off her backpack onto the floor of the cave and dug within it ferociously. She took out the glinting yellow shards of crystal. She approached the great stone and held the shards up to it.

"Please," she whispered. She pressed the shards onto the surface of the stone. They sparkled, and she looked up, and beheld the light far above her, and the rope swayed.

She felt herself fall forward, and found herself splayed onto Fran, who lay still. Vix dashed her eyes about her and looked for the smoke and the great eye. They were gone. The great crystal had split open and began to turn to dust before her.

She quickly worked with Fran to revive her. Her friend's eyelids twitched, and suddenly she took in a great breath and coughed it out. The air spun with tiny golden flecks lit by the distant sunlight.

Vix stroked her friend's forehead and wept silently. Fran began to breathe normally.

"Thank you," Vix said to the air around her. "I'm truly sorry."

The voice returned, but the smoke and the eye remained hidden.

"We have not released you," it said to Vix. "You must still climb away. If you can do that, then you can leave. You cannot take part of us away. And you must never return."

Vix nodded. "I promise," she said, and she put her arm behind Fran's neck, giving her water from her pack's canteen. Fran sputtered.

"Oh no," Fran said hoarsely.

The rope drifted down, sending eddies of topaz sparkles all about the two women, and fell in a soft heap at their feet. The light grew dim suddenly, and Vix and Fran looked up quickly to see the hole above vanish in darkness.

BLUE LANTERN NiGHTFALL

Dala watched the *Blue Lantern*'s flames blast the dust on the landing pad into a high spume. The low cloud deck above flickered briefly, reflecting the flames. That was the only bright light her tired eyes had seen in weeks.

"Engage craft," she commanded into her helmet comms. Trundle, the launchpad bot, responded with a series of musical tones, and rolled forward, skillfully navigating a series of cables now cleared of the weeks of dust since the last landing.

The flames winked out, and steam fizzed out of the rocket. Dala watched Trundle approach the craft. Seven notes from the bot told her that it had cleared the password controls to open the ship.

Groceries, here I come, thought Dala. She exhaled, and the crease between her eyes relaxed just a bit. A ramp lowered with a soft hum, the doorway into the *Blue Lantern* offering Trundle an entry to retrieve the goods. But a shadow filled that doorway.

Dala hissed, "Trundle, reverse and return to me."

Trundle sent questioning notes, and a great arc bounded from the shadow within the ship. Trundle crackled from its attack and slid backwards, and began to spin in place.

Dala backed up. This uncrewed vessel held something. Or someone. In the dark of Europa's landscape, one light now shone forth, an outline in blue, as dusk enveloped the land. And Dala did not know if it might be friend or foe, human…or otherwise. It began to descend, and she froze. Then she began to run. And within seconds, she collided with someone, or something.

"I am here to take you away," it said, and its blurred features confused her, but she felt it reach around her, and she could not escape its grasp.

GALLEON'S WAKE

A glinting vessel shone in the light of two small, yellow binary stars, their light reflected off its cobalt livery, as it swung in a slow arc around a gas giant and its golden moon. Signals stretched like ever-larger ripples through space to reach this ship, but the calls went unanswered, like a spring bird who sings forever but never captures a mate. No springtime would come for this craft, and no landing on a soft world, for it carried death in its hold, and nightmares on its bow.

"*Eryr Glas*, this is Planitia Traffic Control, requesting your status, do you copy?" Iterations of this message looped over and over again and were met with dark silence.

Within its damaged hull, something stretched itself through every vein and conduit of the ship, its hardware, and its wetware, and it cared naught for the inhabitants, their feelings, their souls, or their lives.

Give to us your everything. Why do you not allow us entry? Give to us your everything. Give to us. Give to us.

One hand, gloved, shaking, reached outward from where its owner clung, close to delirium, innards spasming, refuse cycling at maximum.

I've shit myself, Kath thought, absently, glancing below her at the streaming entity curling around like wafts of smoke, eddies from a malice unlike anything she had experienced before. She had discovered what it was, but did not understand it, could not understand it. It had no sense for empathy, and so it was beyond what her mind could comprehend.

The crew had siphoned up the last bit of galetridium, enough to power not only the *Eryr Glas*'s drive, but long tubes within its lower deck as well…enough for a fleet of thousands. And that was the goal, after all. Kath had shoved all that down long ago, before applying to the gig. She was young, mostly unattached (except for the occasional trysts with Nox, when wakefulness and extreme boredom had taken hold of them both), and she didn't think beyond the pay of this gig as a stepping stone to the next. It suited her to go into chill-down, because she could forget, for a time, hands around her neck, fingernails digging in, the flat stare of dark grey eyes not meeting her own. A face she chose not to remember.

Yet out here, the crew, Captain Cavaroc, Madden, Vassey, Dirk, and Nox, along with the drone bots, kept better company for her than she thought she would tolerate. She would look in her small mirror in her bunk, and see only a drawn face, stern in the brow under frizzed brown hair, and a set mouth. Age would have lent her mouth to a dour downturn. But she no longer had that luxury.

The drone bots—Giblet, Truss, and Drumstick—had one by one scanned the moon's canyons. Vassey had sent Truss down at the first sign of paydirt.

"Signal is *strong!*" she cried, punching the air and shimmying in her seat. "Payday!"

An excited whoop from Dirk, a nod of approval from the captain, and everyone else murmuring in relief. Sleep, mine, sleep, mine, then home, then on to the next gig: that was their life, that was Kath's life. Their camaraderie was shallow yet meaningful, the same as in any office with a short-term job.

Truss had returned with its scoopers, and Drumstick had been sent forth to follow. The scoopers transferred the galetridium into the storage tubes as Truss automated the setup. After Drumstick's sojourn, Giblet followed suit. All three of them whizzed back and forth to the golden moon and returned each time to fulfill their jobs. Madden and Dirk checked the samples for purity. Nox made sure they were secure for transport. They were nearly finished, with just one more run from the bots. The bots, however, powered down.

Nox said to the three of them, who sat rotund and squat and still on the storage bay floor, "Get on with you then."

Truss powered on its lights, lifted itself aloft, and slammed into Nox's face, smashing his nose. Yelling and grabbing that wounded organ, Nox did not see Giblet floating near him, and that bot then smashed into the side of Nox's head. Nox fell to the floor. Drumstick barreled down from above, and split Nox's skull.

"What the fuck is going on down there?" yelled Cavaroc in the cockpit. "Nox is offline!"

Kath sat up, electrified, unsure what she had heard. "What—what do you mean, offline?" But Madden and Vassey already pounded along the composite floor down to the bay. Dirk switched the control panels to display the footage of the bay.

"Jesus Christ," he muttered, and he turned back to see Kath just in time. She sank to her knees and let out a small wail. He clambered over to her and picked her up by her armpits. "Kath, Kath—"

More yelling. Dirk whipped his head up and saw the carnage of the bots attacking the other crew.

"Shut them down!" someone yelled through the speakers.

Cavaroc bellowed, "They're not responding! They *are* shut down!"

In the blurred chaos, someone tried to strike the drones, but Cavaroc was right: they did not respond at all, and kept pummeling, and the team members scurried and crawled and tried to get away. Then the ship went dark, and Kath felt herself go weightless.

"What is happening?" she managed to croak, as Cavaroc slammed his fists on the console.

"We've lost auxiliary."

Screams and yells from the bay were all that they could hear; otherwise, an ominous silence stalked through the ship as its engines sat still and dead.

Kath could see something pale in the darkness, something growing brighter. If she stared directly at it, she could not see it. But from the corner of her eyes, it was there, and it snaked its way through the hold. Cavaroc stood oblivious. Dirk fumbled under the console, found what he was looking for, and readied a gun in his left hand.

"Do you see that?" he whispered.

"What?" Cavaroc demanded.

The screams had stopped. No footfalls could be heard.

Just that lilting, palest blue smoke-like haze, twisting and roiling toward them.

Give to us your everything. Give to us. Give to us.

"Who are you?" yelled Cavaroc. "Stand down!"

Give to us. Give to us.

A sickening crack sounded through the cockpit, and Kath felt something wet and slimy splatter her check as it burst past her in zero-G.

"Cap—Captain!" breathed Dirk. Then, "Fuck *you!*" and he began shooting, at what, Kath could not imagine, for how could anyone shoot at smoke?

Kath knew it was not smoke, of course, but she could not fathom it. She watched as it approached her, and she drifted, not moving, only hearing her pulse throttle in her ears. The smoke enveloped Dirk, and entered his mouth, and he yelled one last time, and then he burst from within, his esophagus rupturing outward through his skin as if yanked.

The smoke drifted on.

Give to us your everything. Give to us. Give to us.

"No," said Kath, firmly, knowing she tasted death, as the brains of her captain had slapped into her mouth and she had gagged them back out again. "No. No. *No!*"

Give to us your everything. Why do you not allow us entry? Give to us your everything. Give to us. Give to us.

"No!" she said, firmly, thinking back to her torture, back to the dead-grey eyes that never cared for her pain.

I am facing something unlike anyone has ever seen, and yet somehow, I've seen it before, she thought.

Give to us your everything. Why do you not allow us entry? Give to us your everything. Give to us. Give to us.

Again, "No."

She heard the ship screech, as if a great claw scraped it from outside. It would split the ship open, and she would be sucked away into frigid blackness, and she felt ready.

And then, silence. The smoke vanished.

The lights switched on. The gravity followed, and the slapping and cracking of bodies falling before her echoed in the quiet cockpit.

She trembled and looked down at her hands.

She heard a whirring sound.

A tinny voice chirped, "You are now the captain, Kath Rasey!"

She drew her hand over her blood- and brain-stained face, stared down, and beheld Truss, Drumstick, and Giblet.

"You—killed them," she whispered.

They blinked their lights up at her. "Captain Rasey, what do you command?"

She knew they had been under the entity's control.

"Get us out of here," she whispered. "And," she shuddered, looking about her, and dreading what she might see in the bay below, "clean up everything."

She strapped into the pilot's chair, shivering constantly, and shut down the comms. The engines howled on, and she and the three drone bots hurtled away from the moon, the planet, and the creature. She hoped that "no" had been enough.

INTO THE DARKEST HOLLOW
TALES OF HORROR

THE TUNNEL AT THE END

It stretched in a black arc, a toothless maw into which the road crumbled.

"They said you can hear the screaming inside the tunnel!" whispered Nate.

Sara snickered. "It's just a tunnel. Just drive. Let's get this over with, I have a test tomorrow."

Vic sat at the wheel. The old Mustang sputtered. It had been his grandfather's.

"They've been saying things about this place for years," he said with a grunt. "Don't you think by now we'd know if it was true?"

Nate shook his head.

"Maybe this wasn't such a good idea," he said, his hands gripping the back of the passenger seat.

"Hey!" cried Sara, and the two boys jumped. "Let go of my hair!"

Nate muttered an apology and sat shaking.

Sara, now powerfully annoyed, said testily, "Would you just *go*?" She thumbed her phone. "The reception is bad here. I really need to get back. Either back up and turn around or gun it. It's a short tunnel!"

"How can you tell?" asked Nate.

The inky archway showed no light, no depth. It was just black.

"Because I've been here in the day!" Sara snapped, exasperated. She swung her long, straight, mahogany hair over her shoulder.

"So, you've been through it?" Nate asked.

"No," Sara admitted. "We were in too wide a car. Had to turn around. It's an old tunnel."

"Like, I don't know if this thing is gonna fit," Vic said, his hands rubbing the bumpy steering wheel. "If I scrape the paint, Dad'll kill me."

Sara clucked her tongue and Nate cleared his throat.

"Turn around then," he said.

"Nah," Vic said, his eyes looking straight ahead. "I think it'll make it."

Sara crossed her arms and looked back at Nate.

"We're going," she said, as if that was the final authority.

Nate covered his eyes.

The Mustang growled back to life, and Vic eased it forward.

"Go faster!" said Sara, and in the dim light of her phone, Nate could see her throat bob from swallowing.

"Can't," said Vic. "Having a hard time getting it to go at all!"

Nate gripped the seat again, careful not to catch Sara's hair.

"Then stop! Back up!"

Vic put his foot on the brake.

"It's not stopping!" he said, and he pumped the brakes.

They rolled forward, ever forward, to the black expanse of the tunnel.

Sara cried, "Why can't you stop?"

"I don't know!" yelled Vic.

"I'm getting out!" said Sara, and she tried opening the door. It would not open.

She tried opening the window. It didn't roll down.

"We're going in!" Vic cried out.

Nate breathed harder and faster, pulling at the door handle. Then he leaned back and pushed with his feet and kicked the glass.

All light vanished.

"My phone!" said Sara softly. "It's dead."

"We're in," said Vic, his voice flat.

No light could be found anywhere. They could not see each other. Only the sound of their breathing proved they were together at all.

Then they heard it. A quiet echo at first, it rose in pitch, and met them at last.

A scream.

The scream.

Nate felt tears stream down his face, for he had no control then of his body, and there was no escape. He heard Sara breathing quickly, whimpering. Vic was silent except for an occasional slam of his feet on the gas, which did nothing. The car engine then stopped.

"Let's get out and run back!" Sara said, her voice shaking.

"Can't get the doors open!" said Nate.

Vic repeated his foot pumping on both the gas and the brakes, while trying to turn the car on again. Nothing.

The scream continued to rise in pitch.

Nate reached his hands forward to try and touch Vic or Sara, and he felt nothing. The car began to vibrate.

The scream grew louder.

"What's happening?" Sara yelled.

Then the car lurched, and Nate could feel himself sliding.

"We're falling!" Sara screamed.

The car was falling in empty blackness, falling, falling.

Then all three of them screamed. And screamed. The scream.

STOLEN ART

Julian Broadmoor rapped the doorknocker. He hefted his briefcase, tugged at his scratchy shirt collar, and batted off lint from his tweed jacket. The jacket repelled some of the light drizzle, as did his bowler hat. But it was making its presence known down the back of his neck. He'd left his umbrella behind.

No matter, he thought. *I have everything I need.*

He waited, cast a glance at the lowering sky, and moved closer to the door. The dark grey awning above it arched into a kind of apse, and underneath he could squeeze in just enough to avoid any of the sideways rain as it floated around in the breeze. He knocked again.

A dog yipped somewhere down the street. It was a quiet neighborhood, perhaps over two hundred years old. The manor he stood before looked much older. His papers backed up this observation: it was built in 1657. Its wooden awnings had been replaced over time, but the large grey stone seemed anomalous in this area. No other house looked the same as this. It in fact looked rather like a small castle.

Someone's picture of grandiosity, but not quite.

He noted the wrought-iron fencing around the outside of the hedge, which fanned either side of the front of the manor and extended around the back. That hedge looked severe to him: trimmed within an inch of its life, so as to appear lifeless. Julian doubted any creature would want to dwell there, as it surely formed a dense matrix of impenetrable leaves.

He stood contemplating this, and watching the rain bead on his shoes, when he heard at last the hollow sound of footsteps on a wood floor. A series of clicks and scrapes heralded the door's unlocking. It swung open, and he met someone who looked as if she had walked straight from the dour hedge itself.

She was every bit as boxy, and presumably as boxed in, as the harshly landscaped hedge. Her long-sleeved dress stretched to the floor, where a faint edging of dust could be seen along the hem. Atop the dress, a long, white apron stretched over her broad yet lean frame. That apron looked as if it could stand on its own, owing to the amount of starch applied to it. The woman looked at least seventy, but it was hard for Julian to tell. He recalled a lesson his father had imparted to him long ago: "Never assume a woman's age. Or whether she's with child. Trust me, lad, if you value your life!"

And Julian did.

She stared at him through wire-rimmed glasses, with just the faintest upturn at their corners. *Some personality then*, he mused. Her hair was tied into a knot at the back of her head, and it was pale grey. Her eyes were dark grey, and really the only thing *not* grey about this woman was that alarming apron.

"Hello!" Julian offered a hand, for the woman simply stared at him. "I am Julian Broadmoor, and I am here about the deed."

The woman cleared her throat and reached over to her right. She pulled a cord, and Julian heard a bell echo softly in the distance.

She had not taken her eyes from him the entire time.

"I'll get you some tea, Mr. Broadmoor," she said finally, with a rasping voice that sounded quite as if it had been unused in a century, or perhaps more. "Well, come in then."

Julian obliged, removing his hat. She snatched it and his coat before he could catch his breath. Stowing these out of sight, she reappeared and led him to a parlor.

"Thank you, er—"

"Mrs. Clinkit," came the reply in a chop of syllables.

"Thank you, Mrs. Clinkit."

She waved him toward the open parlor door, and then swept off, presumably to get the tea.

Now, having been accustomed to visiting the homes of elderly patrons, Julian had expected the presence of a parlor. He always looked forward to this, for he felt that parlors, while not indicative of a person's true wealth, often revealed something of one's nature. Typically, there would be at least one artifact that gave him a sense for the person.

Julian walked into that parlor and felt his pulse surge. All along the walls were shelves, and on each shelf, dozens of jars filled with a lurid yellow liquid glinted in the gas lamps. Within each jar floated a human heart.

Julian's reasoned side of his mind thought, *Of course, of course. He was a physician for many years.* But his pulse betrayed his true feelings. *This is macabre. This is ill conceived. This is an obscenity!*

He reeled, and fortunately found a chair close enough that he could slide into. He rubbed his temples. His head ached. He then heard the alarming squeal from the wheels of a teacart, trundling on the wood floors.

Presently Mrs. Clinkit pushed the cart in through the parlor door and over the edge of the rug, which precipitated clinking noises from the cups and saucers.

Julian, in a fit of perhaps madness, thought, *Mrs. Clinkit clinks it!*

And he realized his brow must have shone with sweat, so he flicked out a handkerchief and wiped it. Mrs. Clinkit ignored him completely and set about uncovering the food and pouring his tea.

At any other time or place, the food might have been appetizing to him, and he might have taken it gratefully. As it was, he could not see beyond dozens and dozens of hearts, deep muddy in hue, some outright black, drifting in jars. To him they felt like eyes, they felt alive.

He could only think in profanity at that point, as he tried his best not to vomit.

"Dr. Deneb will see you shortly," Mrs. Clinkit announced, startling Julian.

"I—yes, thank you," Julian stammered. "Thank you for the tea."

She turned to leave, and Julian felt as though he wanted to say something, wanted to ask about those hearts. But she left, and he sat there, facing food and drink he knew he should be grateful for. He found himself stirring his tea and trying unsuccessfully to look *only* at it and not at the denizens on those shelves…

But one of them flashed at him.

He choked on his tea.

He looked again and saw one particular heart in one particular jar. But this was no ordinary heart. It shone, it sparkled. Finally, he felt fortified enough to stand, and so he walked over to the jar.

He was right. It was a jewel, like a great, deep red garnet, suspended in the jar, and in the rough shape of a heart. It was translucent, but so deep a red that one could imagine its being bottomless. He dared to pick up the jar.

A gust of wind blew into the room, chilling his neck. Holding the jar tenderly, he turned. He almost dropped the jar.

Before him stood a shape of a woman, pale, with a long, draping white dress and pale hair tied back with a small braid on each side of her temple. He could see through her to the other side of the room. She held a finger to her mouth.

"Please do not yell," she said, in a voice soft like the wind among pines. "The Wizard will be here soon."

Julian stared, open-mouthed. "The—the Wizard?"

I am asking a ghost about a wizard. Did someone slip me absinthe?

"Yes," she said. "I am...was...Shellany."

Julian blinked at the apparition named Shellany.

"I am Julian," he said, staring at first, then blinking. "Julian Broadmoor. Did—did you say *Wizard?*"

"Yes," Shellany replied. "The Wizard Deneb who lives here. He is the person who stole my heart, which you now hold."

Julian tightened his grip on the jar, for fear of dropping it.

Thinking as logically as he could, given the circumstances, he asked her, "Why is your heart crystalline?"

"The Wizard made it so," Shellany replied, and Julian watched as her hands drifted toward the jar.

"H-how?" Julian replied. *I am asking a ghost how her heart was made crystalline by a wizard. Dear old Dad never had advice for* THIS.

Shellany's hands approached but never touched the jar holding her crystalline heart.

"The Wizard spoke pretty words," she said in her whispery voice. "I enjoyed the pretty words. They made me feel special. He became my suitor, and he treated me to fine foods. He promised me many things. I believed all his words.

"He brought me to his house, which I dared to do, despite how it might have looked. I was entranced by the Wizard, by his generosity, by his grace, by his—"

"His words," Julian finished. He looked at her, and he pitied her. She was beautiful, in an elfin way. What must have she looked like as a living, breathing person?

"Yes," Shellany answered.

Julian looked at all the other hearts. "And...so...whose are those?"

"The Wizard killed them all," Shellany replied, her breathy voice cooling the air between them.

Julian's face went pale.

"They did not interest him. He said I was intelligent, and talented, and beautiful, and full of grace," Shellany explained. "So he wanted to keep me. But not as a partner, as a collectible. I would not be shared with the world. I would not be public with him as his wife. He would only take me out as he wanted me. And the rest of the time, he would set me aside. As a piece of stolen art."

Julian felt a flush of rage stain his face. This man, or Wizard, or whatever he was, he had taken something precious from the world. The Wizard had enchanted Shellany, and who knew how many others, to their doom. Yet he kept Shellany entrapped, his special keepsake.

"I'll kill him!" hissed Julian suddenly. "I'll kill him, and I'll free you, I swear it!"

Shellany's face bore a glorious smile, and her wavering form seemed to glow.

"I knew you would be the one to save me," her soft voice told him.

"There is no saving you," a voice crackled in the air. Julian swung around, and in the parlor, there stood the Wizard Deneb.

The Wizard was tall, so tall that Julian had to bend his head back to look up at him. His clothes were black and overly large, draping over him as if trying to conceal some strange, inhuman shape. His hair was white and his eyes deep-set and black, and his beard was white and neatly trimmed. All in all, he could certainly have passed for a man. But Julian knew in that second, from the dark eyes flickering in the gas lamps, that this was no man.

And Deneb stepped into the parlor, facing Julian and Shellany, who had wafted beside him and refused to leave Julian's side. The Wizard leaned down, grinning, with horrible silver teeth.

"There is no saving either of you."

AUTUMN'S DUSK

Autumn Goggins grew confused by her own footfalls in the slippery fallen oak leaves. She turned about and realized that she had wandered off from her usual path, after dusk painted the sky indigo, and the sickle moon split a pewter cloud above her. A dog barked off in the distance. Autumn took her hands out of her pockets, touched the tip of her nose, and found it cold.

"Now, how did I get here?" she wondered aloud. She stood at the edge of a thicket of dying kudzu, which throttled all the trees in the vicinity save one: the great scarlet oak that stretched its arms over a dank ravine below.

She had been walking for over thirty minutes, having explored her usual spots for her evening walk, and found too much to occupy her mind to pay great attention to the fact that she had circled back toward her house. Along that route, during daylight, she favored a one-lane road that wound back into the forest dividing the finer houses of the ridge from the crumbling homes of the valley where she lived. She had been stressing over money and fretting about her nearly empty fridge. She felt that frenetic edge at the end of the month: Could she make it through without hunger? Could she manage to pay rent on time, or would she need to beg her landlord yet again to extend it a few days? For her employer could not be relied upon to get the pay out in the first place, and on other occasions, the mail had been outright stolen.

She had, in fact, ignored the silly orange pumpkin faces that the wealthy ridge neighborhood liked to place over the lanterns in their front lawns. She walked, fists thrust hard in her pockets, and did not realize until she finally stopped and skidded among the leaves where she had arrived. This path trailed off from her favorite road, and she had often wondered in the tame light of day why the path existed in the first place. She had never wandered here at night before.

It was much too cold for crickets now. Halloween was tomorrow. Soon the hard frosts would prickle the earth and her boots would crunch on the little mud-spikes, like so many tiny stalagmites. She gazed all about her and let out a puff of air. It hung momentarily and then vanished.

Autumn.

She blinked. She instinctively shivered, and shoved her hair deeper into the hood of her jacket. She thought, *I'm tired. I'm hearing things. I need to go home.*

A *shiff* sound in the ravine made the hair on her neck rise. She backed up and away from the edge of that ravine.

Autumn.

She sucked in air, turned around, and found no one. What she did find set her heart thumping: the road was gone. The high-end homes with their elaborate topiary trees and boring red brick were gone as well. She was alone in a dark land and realized that even the soft orange lights of the town on the horizon were missing as well.

Autumn.

She swore under her breath and walked in the direction where the road *should* have been and inexplicably was not. She felt a sudden stabbing pain in her left ear, and clapped her hand instinctively over it. She cried out.

Autumn, why don't you come down here? I need to talk to you.

Autumn quaked. "Look, I don't know who you are, or what's going on, but I'm leaving, you hear?"

Where will you go, Autumn? You are not home now.

"Of course I'm—" she began, but she stopped. *I'm talking to the air. I'm somewhere I shouldn't be. What is happening?*

She rolled her eyes this way and that, and saw no more Halloween lanterns, no houses, and no lights save the crescent moon and the fuzz of starlight between clouds. *What is happening?* And she felt her throat tighten and her eyes sting. *I won't panic. Breathe. Breathe. Think. There's where the road should be. I'm going that way.*

She began trudging forward on the fallen oak leaves, damp from dew already, and skidded as she approached what should have been the lane heading back up to the ridge. From there she could go home.

You are not home now.

Autumn let out a "*Hunh!*" and ran. She thrashed against vines, suddenly slinking down from above, and she heard whispers. They were mixed with the strange voice that came from nowhere yet everywhere in her mind.

Why don't you come down here, Autumn? I need to talk to you.

"Leave me alone!" she shouted, and her voice seemed to suspend. It did not carry. It sounded canned. "Oh God," she whispered. "Where am I, what is happening?"

Just come down here, Autumn, so I can tell you.

"Who *are you?*" Autumn yelled, but even as she raised her voice, its pitch flattened again. She flailed, looking all around her, and at her feet, and vines now stretched like a cage in all directions. The lane—or what had been the lane—was completely blocked now by those vines. And they encroached, shivering, rustling. She stared up and out of them, watching the faint light of stars and moon shrink. She would be entrapped soon in a cone of vines, with no way out.

"Just—please let me go. I need to go home, I need to get back to–"

Autumn, you are not home now.

"I *know* that!" she shrieked, and she tried to look for the oak tree, something, anything that might lend her a mental anchor to time and place. She knew the place, through some shadowed lens, but she began to wonder about the time.

She sat down and hugged her knees. The ground within her cage of vines felt warmer than the air outside of it. She trembled uncontrollably for a few moments, and her lungs rejected this treatment by answering with a bronchospasm. She coughed.

Then she controlled her breath. Shaking at first, she forced air into her lungs and slowly exhaled it, counting to ten. She then stood again, and pushed her hands against the vines. They felt taut and rigid, and try as she might, she could not break them.

Then she felt angry.

"I don't know who you are or why you're doing this," she said loudly, vehemently. "Where do you want me to *go?*"

Come down here, Autumn, so I can tell you.

"I can't very well come down *anywhere* if you've got me trapped, dammit!" she shouted. "Let me out of this shit!"

She noticed, then, that her voice did carry, finally. Emboldened and enraged, she ran at the cage of vines, intending to strike it with her shoulder, but instead, they parted, and she fell fully onto the ground and sprawled. She swore more as she clambered onto her knees. She could see a shadow all around her, a shadow with many arms. She shuddered and made herself look up.

It was the great scarlet oak, bending its arms toward her. She felt her mouth fall open and her lips go dry. Before she could move, the branches creaked and snapped and swirled, and some of them bent down low enough to wrap around her. She felt herself being lifted at least twenty feet into the air, and for a moment she felt weightless. Then, with a rush she saw the ground rising to her, and she thought, *That's it. I'm going to be smashed by a tree. A tree is going to kill me. Well, now I don't have to worry about rent—*

But the tree did not deposit her there. It swooped out and over the ravine, all vines and branches of other trees and planets shuffling away to make room. And then, quite unceremoniously, the tree dropped her about a foot above the ground onto her side. She grumbled and turned, and then she gasped.

A slim form, some four feet tall, stood next to her. It was covered in leaves: oak leaves. It was shaped like a person, but had no eyes, and no mouth that she could see. It did have arms and legs and feet, completely encased in oak leaves. She could not help but stare rudely down at this creature, for her brain could not come up with a better alternative.

Autumn.

She thought for a moment. She said, "Well, so it's you who's…talking with me, but you have no mouth. You're using thoughts?"

Memories.

"Do I…do we know each other?" she asked. The form simply stood there, not moving, arms at its sides.

Autumn, I need to talk to you.

"Okay," she said, rubbing the leaves off her sides and back. "I'm here. Talk to me."

Autumn, you are not home now.

She could not help it, and snorted. "I got that message, loud and clear. But where is my home? What is this, some kind of illusion? A Halloween prank?"

She felt stupid even saying that, because she knew on a core level, perhaps to the very bonds in her DNA, that this was no trick. She was in a different version of place. Of home.

No. You are not home now.

"What do you mean? I do live here."

This is not your home.

Autumn shook her head. "I—don't understand. And who *are* you? Is there someone under those leaves—"

And she reached out for a moment, but the great oak shot a branch down against her chest and flung her back. She thought she heard a deep, baritone *huff* from the tree, but she could not be sure.

Home. And the leaf-being raised one arm and pointed off in a direction. Autumn watched. She crinkled her forehead and thought. Could this being mean…her old home? From years ago, out in the country, by the train tracks?

Home.

"I—okay, yes, I grew up somewhere out there. And," Autumn turned to track the direction of the leafy arm, "yes. It was out to the southwest, near the old station."

I need to talk to you.

Autumn watched the being slowly lower its arm. The oak tree bristled above them.

They told you I moved away.

She blinked. "What? Who told you—who—"

The being continued, *They told you I moved away with my dad.*

Autumn felt a cold spike in her chest, as if she had been stabbed, but she pressed her hands along her sternum and found it quite intact. Her mind began collapsing: flashes of her adulthood, her many moves, her work, her lonely life, her missing the one companion she had had for three years. When she was eleven.

"No," said Autumn, because she did not know what else to say. "No. *Ryan?*"

Everything stilled then: the shuffling of leaves in the night wind, the creaking of the oak, her breath. She remembered. They were sitting against the old chain-link fence. Ryan was leaving to move to Georgia. She was eleven, he was twelve, and this was the moment they said goodbye.

He had come to her one afternoon, after school, not two weeks prior. Shaking, he did not know what to do, tears in his great brown eyes, which his bowl haircut obscured just a bit. He had been her best friend, and then he had moved away with his father. Or so she had been told. She had never met his father; Ryan talked of him in reverent tones, and clearly missed him. His mother seemed nice enough after the divorce, but when the stepfather moved in, everything had changed.

"Ryan—" she began, wanting to reach out to this leaf-child.

This is my home now.

"No, Ryan, what happened, how'd you get here, what is this?" Autumn said all at once.

You are tall now. This is not your home.

"But why are you here, what is going on?"

The leaf-boy began to walk, his feet making no sound, and then he turned and said to her through her thoughts, *Halloween was fun with you. I never told you that.*

Autumn felt her abdomen heave from years of unshed tears. There was much they had never told each other, two kids with sticky popsicle hands coated with tree bark from all the climbing out in the country. Two kids that time and family had seen fit to separate, or so Autumn always believed. Until now. She did not want to know, but she knew she had to.

"They brought you here," she said slowly, "to the ravine. Ryan! Ryan. I'm so sorry. I am so, so sorry. If I'd known, I would have helped—"

We can say goodbye now.

"I don't want to. I'll tell the police, I'll—I'll make sure"—and she gagged on her tears—"you get a proper burial. I'll do whatever I can."

You were my best friend. You were like a sister.

Autumn reached for him, but he walked faster.

We can say goodbye now.

"Is that what you want?" Autumn asked, aching to run after him and throw her arms around him and carry him away from that damp cleft in the earth where he had been thrown so many years ago. But branches seized her from above, and a low, deep sigh resonated from the great oak. She was swiftly raised and placed back above the ravine.

"Ryan, Ryan!" she sobbed.

Now you can go home.

"Wait!" cried Autumn. And she found her voice ringing clearly through the air, and echoing. She gasped and found lights shimmering through the trees: the creamy-gold lights of houses. She heard the same dog barking, more intensely. She glanced over her shoulder, and the manic black triangle eyes and jagged mouth goggled at her from the ridiculous plastic pumpkin lantern of the estate behind her. She turned her gaze back to the oak tree, which looked more decrepit and gnarled than she had remembered.

"Oh, Ryan," she whispered. She set her feet forth though, and with a supercharged strength she walked up the lane, pumping her legs until they burned. She topped the ridge and slipped across the main road, down to the valley toward her house. She startled two cats and set at least five dogs raging. Porch lights tripped on. She made it to the house and threw the door open, slammed it shut, and locked it. She stood with her back against it and looked at her living room, the floors dark and stained, the furniture spare, joyless. No. She would not go on like this, with an empty home and an empty life. She would do that for him. After she found justice for his murder.

She glanced at the clock, and she closed her eyes and swallowed unshed tears. Midnight.

"Happy Halloween, Ryan."

THE GLOVE AND THE BLACK LANTERN

Dear listener, a cautionary tale of woe and strange tidings awaits if you would care to listen to it. But take heed! For if you, weary traveler, wish to sleep as soundly as the soft doves outside your bedroom window, you might recoil from these events that transpired not long ago.

It began with a note nailed upon a lamppost, in a rather crude manner, with a rather crude and rusted nail. But no matter: Calliope Windsor saw the notice, and therein the trouble started.

Miss Windsor found herself by that very lamppost just recently, mere weeks ago, dear listener. And had decorum and common sense not escaped her at that moment, this tale might not ring with the notes of tragedy and mystery on high.

Consider the setting: an afternoon, half-past four, in which Miss Windsor decided upon a shortcut by Orion Cemetery, rather than taking the walk through the park to the quay back to her brownstone. This was an hour which, in late springtime by the sea, glowed golden upon the edges of the newborn leaves, and when shadows remained periwinkle in hue. In all areas of comportment, Miss Windsor was not in the wrong by taking a detour. She erred, however, in not taking an escort along.

The paper, only slightly curled at the corners, clearly had not endured the rains of the prior week, so she could see that it was new. And it had been placed at just the right time and at the right height to catch her hazel eyes, which at the golden hour looked amber flecked with green. What, dear listener, turned her head and caused her to walk that way? We may never know for certain, but whispers tell us perhaps some clues.

Something changed Miss Windsor's mind, and as it happens, not only hers.

Ellington, the maid of all work in the Windsor home, had seen Miss Calliope off at the post office. Calliope, by the maid's own account, had delivered three sealed letters to be mailed. Rather mysteriously, thought Ellington, Calliope had not told her maid what they contained. She had smiled in her dreamy, twisted-mouth way, adjusted her gloves, and walked out onto the platform and along the street. Ellington recounted the need to purchase food for the night's dinner, and so bade Miss Windsor farewell. Oh, the tremulous tones of regret Ellington has used since, remembering that instance in its recent, crystalline clarity, a clarity only seen in a time of deep regret, when another decision might have meant the difference between seeing Calliope Windsor at dinner that night…or never again!

You may wonder what had steered Calliope aside from her track. Did someone urge her? We can only piece together the words of witnesses, of which there are regrettably very few. Aside from the forlorn and, it must be said, at times histrionic recollections of that fateful day by Ellington, there are but three others who are known to have seen Calliope Windsor. Each tale grows stranger by the telling, as you will hear.

"I saw her plain as day," declared a fishmonger who, at the behest of the investigator, we shall call Morris. "Wearin' a straw hat, green ribbon and that, and long dress. No, I don't recall the color. Not one for the fineries of ladies, what. The gloves, aye, they were green like the ribbon on the hat, that I know. Since she'd left one behind."

Upon questioning, Morris insisted that a young woman had walked up to the aforementioned lamppost and taken the sheet of paper nailed to it, but upon pulling the paper off, her glove became stuck by the nail that held it up. She cried out softly, and Morris had turned his head to see what had happened.

"Are you all right, Miss?" he had called out. She had jumped, turned her head, and slipped him a little smile. She waved with her other hand, which held the paper, but the gloved hand had turned red at the fingertips, presumably from her finger being nicked by the nail. She had looked this way and that, and seeming to be in a fit of indecision, removed the bloody glove, and discreetly let it fall to the ground. Morris later found it and placed it upon the lamppost's neck.

Oh, but dear listener, that is not all that happened with that lamp. As Morris touched that glove, stained with blood as it was, and it pressed to the post of the lamp, the panes of the lantern turned pitch black! Being a fisherman, Morris believed staunchly in the tides and in superstition, and he looked to and fro to see if anyone else had noticed the anomaly. He held the glove briefly in his hand, and feeling a deep chill, as he himself admitted, he placed the glove back on the lamppost and retreated to his stall to close up before nightfall.

"'Twasn't anythin' like I'd ever seen before, and I hope to never again," Morris told the investigator. Visibly shaken, Morris had held his hat in his hand, his crinkled purple-red lips twitching under the grey and gold mustache. After being released from his questioning, Morris decided to move his business farther down along the quay and never to return to the lane near Orion Cemetery.

Ah, and that is not all that happened after that bloody glove touched the lamppost! If Morris had looked down, he would have witnessed something else strange indeed: tiny black cracks in the cobblestone, radiating out from that lamppost like forked spokes on a dark axle. Yet apparently one boy *did* see the cracks form, just as he skipped by, his pocket full of cockles and his ginger hair blazing in the lowering sunlight.

"I saw her, yeah!" he squeaked. "I had to get back to me mum, though, didn't I? Else she'd tan my hide, wouldn't she? But I saw the lady, yeah! She was real pretty. She looked like a…like a daffodil!"

This boy, Ralphie, had a mother quite ruddy of face, with frizzled red hair, who glared sternly at him over such a mutinous strain of poetry bursting forth from her son's mouth.

"Now, don't you be getting fancy, Ralphie," she admonished, and the poor lad turned positively scarlet.

The investigator pressed the boy, gently, and under the wary eye of the mother, who held certain renown for bellowing her son's name every afternoon to be sure he could hear her across multiple blocks. Everyone within those blocks could hear her trumpeting lungs as well.

Ralphie bit his lip, hands pulsing in his threadbare pockets, and legs kicking nervously under his chair. "She didn't have nobody with her, sir, honest. The only other person I saw was old Morris. I'd bought some cockles off him, yeah! But that weren't the oddest thing. Besides her being alone and that. It were the ground all around there. There was a sort of popping sound, and then these little cracks all spread out from the lamppost, even under my feet! She musta seen them too."

The mother glared with her eyes squeezed nearly shut, and Ralphie gave a nervous laugh before saying, "Then the lady went on down alongside the cemetery, honest. She turned the corner at the end of the block and that's all I saw of her. Yeah!"

The trail might have gone cold, dear listener, were it not for the final witness on that unfortunate yet beautiful afternoon. Ralphie had spoken as honestly as he could, despite his outlandish claims of cracks in the pavement, but to be sure, our fair city is known for having a few…if not in quite the same uncanny manner as those. For along the southern side of Orion Cemetery, which if you recall was constructed nearly two centuries ago, there was a corner flower shop across the street that belonged to Matilda Dewberry. To the east next door, a milliner had closed shop for the day, but Mrs. Dewberry had lingered a bit to attend to the shop display and bring in the buckets of flowers that had not sold.

To hear Mrs. Dewberry tell it, one Miss Calliope Windsor had turned the corner, holding a piece of paper in her left hand, gloved all in green. Her right hand bore no glove and was balled into a fist. A highly unusual sight for a lady, but Miss Windsor had approached Mrs. Dewberry.

"I'm terribly sorry," she had said, her face stained in the cheeks with a deep rose, but whether from embarrassment or fever, or some unnamed emotion, Mrs. Dewberry could not tell, "but I've cut my finger. Have you a ribbon I can bandage my hand with? I don't want to soil my handkerchief."

"There, there, deary," Mrs. Dewberry had told her. "Let's have a look and get you patched up." She had gestured for the young woman to enter the shop, but Miss Windsor stood firmly outside.

"If you don't mind," she had stammered, her eyes darting back down the direction she had come, "I have a delicate nose around the flowers, though they are most beautiful. I would like to stay outside."

Mrs. Dewberry had paused at the strange request, but nodded gently, her hair taut in a grey bun, her solid and boxy build covered in a soft brown apron lightly streaked with the green dye of plant stems. She brought forth a strip of white muslin and a wet cloth and cleaned the wound.

"You might want to set that paper aside," the woman told Calliope. She could not see what was on the paper, as Miss Windsor had turned it face down against her skirt. That struck her as a bit strange, but then, Mrs. Dewberry respected others' privacy, unlike some folks along the harbor. It must be said, listeners, that Mrs. Dewberry greatly laments not finding out what the paper held up on it.

"Deary, you might want to have that looked at in the morning," Mrs. Dewberry had told her, for the wound was most puzzling. It was a puncture, yet out from it radiated tiny black marks, like legs of a spider, with the wound as its body. The muslin bandage covered the puncture, but the black marks emerged from the edges. "Was it a rusty nail, deary?"

Miss Windsor did not look at Mrs. Dewberry and instead said, "I don't recall," and her eyes seemed glassy and reflective.

"Shall I call someone to escort you to a carriage?" Mrs. Dewberry asked.

"No, no, I'll be quite all right," Miss Windsor had said, patting the bandaged hand gratefully. She had offered Mrs. Dewberry some coins, but the florist had refused. "Thank you for your troubles. I am headed home."

My listeners, I regret to inform you that Miss Windsor did not make it home. She did not make it anywhere, and no one that walked along the path she took has seen her since.

But something else most peculiar occurred after that meeting. Mrs. Dewberry had watched Miss Windsor walk along the eastern edge of the cemetery, toward the waterfront, presumably to catch one of the carriages that regularly passed there. A crashing sound had distracted the florist, however, and she had returned to her shop to see what had happened. She looked around and found three buckets of flowers overturned, their water spilled out from them, only it was not clear water: it was red. She had not yet binned the bloody rags with which she had cleaned Miss Windsor's wound. But that water looked every bit as though it were bloody. It flowed out of the shop and into the gutter of the street and seeped into tiny black cracks all in the cobbles.

And here we reach a most puzzling moment in our shadowy tale: a moment in which no one else witnessed Miss Windsor, yet also when several quite perplexing things occurred.

Shop owners shuttered their shops, turning their signs to "closed," drawing their curtains. Residents above the shops opened their windows to air the scents of cooking onto the streets below, and all went as it did every single day along these quiet streets, where nothing really ever happened aside from the occasional drifter from the waterfront taking a wrong turn.

Ah, but listener, it was no drifter who took a wrong turn on this golden afternoon. It was a young lady, much admired, "out" in society yet a tad eccentric, prone to daydreaming, reading novels, and writing poetry. She adored cemeteries, where, as she had described to a scandalized Ellington once, "Nobody can disturb you there; you can say anything you like without fear of reprisal. It is the perfect place to be listened to."

And what an ominous thing to recollect for poor Ellington. For who *was* listening to Miss Calliope Windsor on that April afternoon? Was it the unturned dead under hillocks of green, with shoots of new flowers poking up from their quiet rest? Or was it something deeper than they, something darker, something older…something not of the world of flower shops and clinking boat masts and little boys with pockets of cockles? For something dark percolated there, between the cracks of the cobbles; something seeped up from somewhere else entirely…

Yet the evening commenced. The lamplighters drifted in and out among the lamps like oversized bumblebees visiting their favored flowers before sunset. So it was every day, still in the golden hour, before it became too dark to do their work and to prevent any pedestrians from taking a tumble either from turned heel or turned drink, as it were. On this day, however, one particular lamp stood out in the fading light.

A young lamplighter by the name of Geoff, chipper, bow-legged, whistling, and covered in soot, had turned the corner of the western side of Orion Cemetery, and walked toward the lamplight where Miss Windsor had plucked the piece of paper from its post and then walked off to an uncertain fate. His eyes fell upon a pale *something* dangling from the lamppost that was his quarry. He tooted off some tunes between his pursed lips, and advanced upon the lamp. He shoved his beret back on his head, his light brown hair clinging to his sweaty forehead.

"Well, what's this?" he said aloud, reaching out to the thing. He pulled at it and held it up in the fading light. "A glove!"

And not just any glove, he realized, but a lady's, and fairly fine in construction; much finer than his sister's, and a soft, spring green. Its forefinger was ripped and stained with blood, and still slightly damp. He puzzled over the glove, and ultimately dropped it so he could set about his work. He noted an old nail and leaned in to look at it. "Ah, it nipped her, did it?" he muttered to himself. He could see just a bit of blood on the head of the ancient nail. He sighed and shrugged and was about to light the lamp.

He heard a swishing sound behind him, and puzzled by it, he turned to look. There he beheld such a strange thing that it took him a full minute or two to react, and react he did. The ground, where the glove had fallen from his hands, had splintered around the thing in twisting cracks like black lightning forks. But that might not have been the strangest thing he witnessed. No, indeed, his evening was about to become even stranger.

The glove *moved*. And not only did it move, it shivered along the ground beneath the lantern. Geoff leapt backward and stared at the thing, mouth agape.

"Geoff!" someone called, and he yelped, and jumped a few inches into the air. "Get 'er lit, will ya? I've got a pint with my name on it waiting at Meb's, so get with it!"

Geoff wanted to say something in retort, but his voice cracked, as if he were a young lad again, rather than a young man of twenty. The glove twitched again, and Geoff's hair rose from its dampened spot on his neck and brow.

"B-bloody rats," he said aloud, as if deciding then and there that the glove was covering a rat, who planned to make off with it to its den somewhere, and make perhaps the most elaborate rat nest material of all time; Geoff thought all of this within seconds, for it made sense to him, somehow, more than anything else. And certainly, more than what happened next.

He shivered, tossing off as much of the strangeness as he could, and turned to light the lantern. He found the panes of the lantern were solid black.

"Who put this one out this morning?" he called to his friends. "Left a right mess, you did! Can't you have cleaned it? Can't even see light out the sides!"

He reached up and, with a towel he'd had around his belt, tried to wipe the black surface of the lantern. He drew back the cloth, expecting to see soot, but even in the lower light, he could see that not only was there no soot on the cloth, but there was also a copious amount of what looked like blood. He jumped backward again and flung the cloth forward, away from him.

"Oh, come on, will you!" cried his friend.

"There's—there's blood," Geoff began. Phil, the friend calling impatiently, stomped over to him.

"Geoff, light the lantern and let's go! All I wanted was *one pint*, mate! One!"

Geoff pointed from the lantern to the cloth.

Phil squinted at the stain. "Oil," he said definitively.

"Oil!" exclaimed Geoff. "On a gas lamp? You've lost it!"

"Have I?" snapped Phil. "I'm not the one mooning around talking about blood when there's a *beer* waiting at the pub, am I? It's an old lantern, and it's filthy. Now light the thing and let's go."

Geoff dropped the towel and looked back at the lantern. He took a deep breath, huffed it out, and lit the lantern. It sputtered, and he felt sure it would go out, but it did not. It did, however, reek of something most foul…something fetid, like a dead animal mixed with the scent of rotting apples. He closed the pane of the lantern, and it flickered within like a blinking, ruby eye.

He shuddered and backed up. He looked around for the glove, and thought he saw something out of the corner of his eye, crawling along the ground. He felt sick. Phil had already stomped off and could be heard swearing, his colorful words echoing in the shallow canyon of the buildings. Geoff shook his head, wiped his hands on his pants, and bolted after his friend.

The sun set, and the lantern glowed dark red, lighting just barely the dark cobblestone streets that encircled Orion Cemetery. The denizens of that fair and verdant space did indeed rest, but outside their protective gate, something oozed up from beneath. It slinked along. It met the abandoned glove, and it teased its tongue around the bloody fingertip, even as the glove itself shifted of its own accord. The something moved quietly, shunning the worms and insects and rodents of the streets that instinctively sprang away from it, and it moved intentionally around the base of the lantern. It bubbled up with a soft and low laughter, twisting and coiling through the cheap form of matter it encountered. It eased its way up the lamppost. The night then grew still and quiet, and a fog settled into the harbor.

In the morning, the street cleaners found nothing amiss along the street there. The lamp had gone out in the night at some point. Its panes looked dark brown in the morning sunlight. There was a glove, stained with blood, that an officer later found alongside a drain. Walking back toward the lantern, the officer discovered the nail, and the dark stain upon it had streaked in the foggy night. A strange and noisome smell emitted from the lantern, so he opened it to look within.

He shouted, and fell back, and held his chest, and Mrs. Dewberry found him gasping there, pointing upward. She stood and looked inside the lantern, and a shriek escaped her, a clarion call of primal alarm that woke the area for blocks around, a scream that said without saying anything, "Danger."

For within the lantern there sat two perfect, hazel-gold eyes, staring out, as if made of glass, and nothing more.

Listeners, a piece of paper was found blowing in the cemetery this morning. It bore a hole in its top, a puncture, and a stain of blood. And on this paper, there could be found a sketch of one Miss Calliope Windsor, with the words "MISSING" all along the top.

LOVE AND OTHER MOMENTS

TRACES OF THE HEART

THE RIVER OF RUBIES

The ruby-glittered river I wend along churns and twists, slows and eddies. It carries me north, along the sea…but never to it. I am on the 405, headed to Los Angeles, and my heart pulls me through this slow current. Brake lights become scarlet jewels in this tributary of wishes.

I look up and a bit east, and I see the pastel little smear that will resolve into white letters that say "HOLLYWOOD." And although my dreams would take me there, reality does not. I am lulled along by the promise of something, of someone, whose mark upon the gilded streets was made by words.

So we danced by the tapping of keys, over many months, and today is the day I drive to him for the first time. It takes three and a half hours from San Diego, and the irony is that I left behind a more chaotic traffic scene there. In LA, the driving skill is comparatively high, because the use is constant. And so there is a predictable undulation. I hear it is much maligned, but perhaps because I have driven in ice and sleet and snow and tornadoes and dust storms on my many road journeys in this country, I find the pace of the City of Angels appealing.

I look to the north again. I climb the hills to reach the 101, and then I head west, heart in my mouth. While I would take this journey again, this is the first time I took it for love. And every time after, I would look to the hills, from my slow coursing, surrounded by so many people…and I would wonder, are you here for dreams? Or necessity? Or heartbreak? Or love?

And I keep driving.

VALENTINES FROM THE PIT

Farrah Banks thumbed through her texts. She rolled her eyes at two, snorted at one, and pushed out her lower lip in disappointment at another.

"Can't make it, sorry, hon," her bud Mack sent. "Jeff surprised me with last minute reservations."

"Lol I forgot it's my mom's birthday, oops," came Sam's message.

"Not sure I'll be able to," texted Millie. She had no prepared excuse.

"Sorry," wrote Finn.

It was the last one that stung the most. Not because she harbored a massive crush for Finn...although that certainly contributed. It was the clipped nature of it. No excuse, no nothing. She used to count on Finn to be at every event.

Farrah looked at the spread of ingredients she had bought for her Great Chocolate Party. Her phone chimed again, and again, and she sighed. More declines. She began putting the ingredients back in the pantry.

Another Valentine's Day with no one to share it with, she thought. *Can't someone share it with me?*

She had got by with chocolate parties and sometimes girls' nights. She reassured herself it was a stupid candy maker and greeting card industry fabrication that meant nothing. Yet here she was, and this deep core of sadness grew in her. It stretched from her throat to her navel.

She reached back in for the chocolate chips she had just put away, intending to pour a fistful and throw them back into her mouth. But the doorbell rang.

Farrah had not installed a door camera, for which her friends admonished her, saying in low tones that it was a good idea. Her housemate traveled frequently, and just now he was away. She never answered the door if she didn't know who was coming.

But she had heard a little *thump*, and then realized there must be a package waiting. She hadn't ordered anything. She hesitated. She looked out the peephole and saw no one. Her phone kept chiming with all the declining texts for her party. Gritting her teeth, she finally opened the door.

On the doormat, there rested a gorgeous heart-shaped box, wrapped in magenta swirls of satin. It was a large Valentine candy box, or so it appeared to Farrah. There was no note attached.

She lifted it into her arms, closed her door, and locked the bolts. She set the beautiful box on her small kitchen table. Her phone kept chiming, and at first she ignored it. But then she thought maybe someone could have texted her saying they'd sent her the box.

But no: a quick scroll through her messages only irritated her more. *Happy Valentine's Day to me*, she thought, frustrated. Then she turned her eyes back to the immaculate box. And her spirits rose.

Aloud, she said, "This is the prettiest box of chocolate I have ever seen."

Nobody seemed to make this kind anymore. She had vague memories of elaborate lacy and velvety Valentine boxes for her mother, when Farrah was a little girl. Back when her own mother had named her for someone beautiful…someone she would never look like. But this one? It was exquisite, its lush satin tucked into rose shapes.

Farrah felt giddy. *Something went right!* she thought.

She couldn't stand another minute. She opened the box. Inside, a heart-shaped cover rested above the contents. The cover itself sparkled in a million hues, or maybe more: iridescent glitter, only it *moved*. It shimmered and flowed, like sunlight glinting on a quick stream. In fact, she could almost hear the water…

And she fell.

She fell right into the heart-shaped box, headfirst, through swirls of glitter and blurs of rainbow color. She had one brief moment to wonder, *Did I eat one of the candies and I'm high?*

And then she landed. In water, in darkness, on hard stone. The only light around her came from the heart-shaped iridescent cover, which lay on the ground beside her. It shone upward, and she looked above her, and saw only stalactites dripping.

Her wrists hurt from softening her most unexpected fall. She stood, and her jeans were damp in the rear. She rubbed her hands together to remove dirt and grit. She felt cold and sore and stunned. Yet that glorious, rainbow-sparkly heart shape shone. She did not know what else to do, so she reached down to pick it up.

It was dark on one side, but the other provided glorious light.

What is happening? she managed to think.

She held out the heart to look around her, and it shown like a lamp through the darkness of the cave. This at first reassured her. At least she could see. She turned one way, and the light shone into the distance. Then she turned the other way.

Light reflected in a thousand eyes, staring at her.

She felt her body go tense, and she tried to breathe, and the air pinched in her chest, and all she could do was moan at first, for nothing else would come out; but she wanted to scream.

A slow shuffling sound met her ears, and the eyes advanced.

Making a panicked sort of bark, Farrah turned. With her Valentine lamp, she fled the other way. She stumbled and scraped herself, and hit her head on stalactites, and splashed through puddles, propelled by the madness of fear.

Finally, her chest hurt so much she had to stop for a moment. She wept silently as she slowly turned the glowing heart behind her. And there they all were: eyes, eyes beyond number, eyes of all sizes. She squawked, and turned to run again, and then found her legs meeting nothing solid, and she fell and bumped and slid.

She landed at last, clutching the heart-lamp to her chest. Its light radiated into the darkness, and she could see something dim, another light source. She swung her heart-light upward, and no eyes danced there. She took a deep breath, and stood in pain.

She walked toward the light source, which was so faint that she imagined there must be only two photons coming from it. But it grew, and she could see, by and by, a more defined path.

I don't know what's there, but it's better than the eyes, she reasoned.

A notch in the stone of the cavern led to a vast opening, so she walked through, and then stood with her lips parted in stupor at what she saw.

There stood a high dais, built of horns and teeth and talons, and glinting with raw jewels of many colors. On this dais sat a throne of opal, which shimmered even more than the heart in her hands. And on this opal throne, a figure reached its head forward to look at her better.

It was immensely tall, perhaps nine feet, perhaps more. Its muscles rippled, but the hands with their long fingers betrayed a great age. Its skin looked deep purple in the light, and its long, straight hair shone magenta: the exact hue of the Valentine box cover. The face!

In the lines of the face, a sharp nose and a strong brow framed eyes that glowed like fading embers in a fire. Something resembling a smile formed on this etched face.

Its voice, lustrous and melodious, spoke to her:

"You received the gift," it said.

Farrah gulped.

"Yes," she said, and she felt her sweaty hands loosen on the heart. "Who are you? And where am I?"

"I am Lord Vatenite," he replied. "You are in my realm. Step closer, Farrah Banks."

Farrah's hair stood up on her neck.

"How do you know me?" she asked.

And she would have liked to run away, but could not. She felt compelled to walk to the lord.

Lord Vatenite stood then, and walked down the steps of his dais to meet Farrah. He loomed over her from his great height, and stared with his fiery eyes down into her face, with her jaws clenched.

"You asked for me," said Lord Vatenite.

"I didn't," Farrah protested.

"Yes, you did," said Lord Vatenite. "You asked quite distinctly, 'Can't someone share it with me?' Referring, of course, to this preposterously overblown holiday you humans adore flagellating yourselves with."

Farrah opened her eyes so wide that she feared they might pop right out and roll onto the ground.

"Did I die?" she asked helplessly. "Is this hell?"

And Lord Vatenite threw back his magenta hair and laughed, which echoed through his great chamber. Startled bats rustled above them.

"Farrah," said Lord Vatenite, "in all your years, you have imagined the perfect day. It is always the same day. It is today. There is chocolate, there is adoration, you are valued. You thought no one cared. But I did."

Stunned, Farrah asked, "Why me?"

Lord Vatenite waved his hand and a tray appeared, laden with dozens of chocolates and flowers and two goblets filled with a violet drink.

"Will you sit with me?" he asked her. "I have made you everything you wanted on this day, over the years. Even the strange little candy hearts. I would very much like to share them with you."

"Why?" Farrah repeated.

Lord Vatenite looked down at her.

"It is dark in the pit, and I like it this way; else I would not have volunteered to rule it so long ago," he told her, with little sparks flying off his eyes. "You were always trying to find a cave when you were growing up, and sometimes you succeeded. Your friends were always frightened, but you were not. You were never afraid in the dark. And you were kind, and generous, and you wanted your friends not to feel lonely on Valentine's Day."

Farrah, unsure how to respond, simply nodded.

Lord Vatenite continued, "I watched your sadness when your friends fell away," and Farrah felt her cheeks go hot. "While I do enjoy it down here, sometimes it is a little boring. And your parties looked like such fun."

"So…you've watched me my whole life?" asked Farrah.

"Oh," laughed Lord Vatenite, "not every moment. But when someone enters my realm, I take notice of their lives, and how they live them. Yours is extraordinary. What you do matters."

Farrah wrinkled her nose. "I've never felt that way. I just wanted to make chocolate treats and share them."

"You have done much more than that," countered Lord Vatenite. "You helped me believe in true kindness. One forgets, over the ages, what that is like. Thank you, Farrah Banks. Now, will you share the treats with me?"

Farrah felt a deep happiness. She looked up at Lord Vatenite, who gestured at the tray of goodies. He picked up one of the candy hearts, and it looked tiny in his large, purple hands. He held it out to her, and she took it. She read it and laughed.

It said, "Be Mine."

SCREENS IN BETWEEN

A pale-blue aura framed Thilly's face, as she leaned in toward the monitor. Beaumain's eyes looked tired, but they lit up at the sight of her, and he rubbed his ginger beard.

"Hello," he said, smirking.

"Hello," she replied, twitching a coil of hair over her shoulder nervously.

"I like your hair," he said.

"I like your beard," she said.

And so the chat began, many hours and a world apart, a meeting at the end of the world.

But seasons change, and the world may end, but a new one rolled on, and so they drifted. A brief check-in here and there. Moments of praise.

"Are you okay? The world has ended, but I still think of you from time to time."

"I am okay, but I am tired, and I worry for my children."

"Yes, I worry for mine as well. It is one thing if I become ill, but if they do…"

And possibilities became impossible. Or so they seemed at first.

"We make things," Thilly wrote in a text one night. It would have been early morning for Beaumain.

"We do indeed," he wrote back.

Thilly stared at her phone and tapped her chin with her fingernail.

"What if we made a way out of this?" she asked.

"What do you mean?" Beaumain wanted to know.

"I mean…what if we made a way to see each other. One that didn't risk our lives. One that is quiet and calm…no stress of travel. We just…*make the way*."

Beaumain adjusted his glasses and grinned, and because he liked indulging her, he said, "Go on."

Thilly said, "You've told me you dream a lot. So do I. What if…what if we met there? Somehow?"

Beaumain shrugged. "I don't see how that would work, but…"

"We'd make it work. Let's try it. I'll think of you right as I'm going to sleep. Set your timer; you'd be just waking up, but still in a dream state."

Thilly took a quick selfie and sent it to Beaumain, and he could see her hair was wild, her face pale from her phone's light, but most of all, her expression radiated hope and possibility.

Could we do that? Could we really? And then he breathed in deeply, for all he wanted in the world just then was to hold her, at the end of all things, but she was so far away.

"I want to try," he said to her. And she bit her lip and smiled.

That night, she curled up in her bed, the night so cold that she kept her socks on. She felt alone, and chilled, and wanted nothing more than to hold him right now. But he was so far away.

I'm thinking of you, Beaumain, I'm thinking of you. Are you thinking of me? Right now? On the other side of the world…away from a text or video? We are under the same moon…I would like to see you there.

And Thilly fell asleep.

She tossed and turned a bit, her body settling in, and then her mind bubbled off, and created the usual strangeness of the beginnings of dreams, in which colors seem different and one's home is the same but not one's own.

Throughout this, she could still hold on to conscious thought, just barely.

"Are you there, Beaumain?"

The dream shifted, and she felt a sense of loss, of regret. *He's not there.* And she walked in a large, cold house, opening dark doorways, smelling soot and mold. But there was one doorway down the hall…a hall unfathomably long. The doorway stood ringed in light. She could hear her shoes scuffing. Other doors on either side of her began to open, and ash-colored arms reached out of them, trying to draw her in, and she tried to run from them. But she could only shuffle.

So long, so long it seemed, this hallway, this interminable distance just to open a door…yet she endured and kept on, the fleshy fingers clawing at her. She could almost feel the warmth of that light ahead.

"Thilly?" a far-off voice called. *"Are you there?"*

Thilly gasped and broke into a run, or what she could do in this netherscape that came closest to a run. Hands brushing her back, tugging her hair, she dared not look behind her. She threw herself against the door. The light shining around it lit her trembling hands, and she found a doorknob.

"I'm here."

She turned the knob, and it opened, and instead of a bright light, there was a simple fireplace crackling in the background. And in the foreground, a man stood there, his beard glowing like embers, his eyeglasses slipping down his nose so that he could look at her. It was Beaumain.

She leapt forward, and he seized her about her waist, and the door with its unwelcome host behind it shut hard. She fell forward and breathed Beaumain in, brushed her fingers through his beard, and he wound his hands all through her waving hair and caressed her neck.

"You're real," she whispered.

"You're real," he answered, and they held each other's faces and their lips met at last.

An explosion of light and color blossomed about them, as if every flower that frost had bitten back in the world at last bloomed again, swirling and twining them together.

"So we can do this now," Thilly managed to say, her smile shaking.

"And now is all we have," Beaumain answered.

FAR APPALACHIA
TALES FROM THE ANCIENT MOUNTAINS

THE QUEEN AND THE MOUNTAIN LAUREL

Laurel was given her name by her pappaw. She was a pale infant, and when her mother and father were arguing what to name her, Pappaw stepped in.

"She looks like a mountain laurel blossom," said Pappaw, squinting his rheumy eyes at her. And so Laurel was named.

She would go with her father on excursions to one of the mountains in Tennessee, to find scraggly, forgettable plants and bring them home to fill out their wooded yard. It had been a year, and now the time had come. The frost had ended in the valleys, but the mountains might still harbor pockets of ice. She thought they were little secret snow villages, where the ice fairies dwelt.

Laurel bumped in her seat in the old Ford Bronco. Her dad drew on his cigarette and swung his arms to and fro, steering over the ruts in the road up Mullins Mountain. He flicked the ashes out the rolled-down window.

They traveled this way a few miles. It exhausted Laurel. But they had bologna sandwiches, an RC Cola, and some chips. She was just about ready for those.

Finally, they pulled into a familiar area, where the road tumbled uncertainly through young spring weeds, past a fire tower. She could feel the chill of the shade the minute she got out of the truck. Her dad handed her a burlap bag, and he grabbed a spade from the back.

The wind whipped up and around them, and she shivered. They walked toward the forest, where hemlocks whirred and hissed. Her dad knew where to go. The year before, they had followed the path of a large creek that spilled from the springs near the mountain's peak. She slipped and slid among the rocks of the creek as she hopped across them, while her father made his way along the bank.

The mountain laurel looked, at first glance, like wildly misplaced mangroves, flung into the air from warmer climes. Their dark, oblong leaves looked like the bay leaves her mom would add to bean soup. In a couple of months, the mountain laurel would bloom into creamy, blush-tinted pom-poms. Less refined than showy rhododendrons, and leggier than azaleas, mountain laurels were the unsung fair ladies of the southern Appalachian forest.

Laurel heard a *ca-chuck* as her dad plunged a shovel into the earth.

A voice whispered to her, "Don't let him."

Laurel jumped from her seat on a cold stone and skidded nearly into the creek. She looked around. The sun shone through the evergreens in a long silver shaft. She could see the form of a tall woman standing next to her, diaphanous, as if made of the sunbeam itself.

"Who—who are you?" Laurel asked in a hushed tone.

The light-lady said, "I am the Mountain Queen. The mountain laurels are my ladies-in-waiting."

Laurel, never a subtle child, said, "I thought they were just plants!"

The Mountain Queen dipped her head, which sparkled like the dappling of late afternoon sun on the surface of quick water.

"No, child. They are like you, but they move more slowly," said the Mountain Queen. And Laurel gazed over at the plants, and gasped. The tall shrubs bowed to the Queen.

"Please, let them be," pleaded the Mountain Queen. "Tell your father."

"He won't believe me," said Laurel. "He says I tell too many stories."

"Try," begged the Queen.

Laurel sighed, nodded, and clambered up to the bank of the stream. Her father was struggling with his digging.

"Daddy," she said to him, noticing his sweat. "Don't take them this time, Daddy."

"What?" he asked, staring at her. "We drove all this way."

"I know, Daddy," said Laurel, and she glanced over her shoulder, and could see the Queen swaying in the weak forest light. "It's not right, Daddy. We have enough of them at home. Please, Daddy. Let's just eat and hike and go home. Please?"

Her father shoved his sunhat up his high forehead and stared down at her brown eyes from his hazel ones. Laurel felt nervous. They had come a long way, after all.

"Well, Laurel," he said to her. "If you feel that way. I guess we have all the laurels we need at home, because we've got you."

"Thank you, Daddy," said Laurel, smiling.

She looked back at the creek and could see the flickering Mountain Queen curtsy. And then the Queen vanished, leaving only her ladies-in-waiting, bowing before them.

MiSTER GERALD

Mr. Gerald terrified us.

Jay and I would return home from illicit bicycling adventures and deliberately press ourselves against the creaking wooden railroad bridge as far as we could, hoping Mr. G would not see us.

A whiff of heat-melted creosote on the bridge slats and the distant, metallic buckling sound of a coal train centered us in time and place. It was 1985, and the broad expanse of summer lay ahead.

We had it all planned out. We would bushwhack The Path, finally, and figure out what beckoned at the end of it, down by the ravine next to the tracks. There was a new empty lot close by, and that meant scouting for ramps to pop wheelies on with our bikes. I had staked out a new, huge tree over in the cow pasture for us to climb. But our primary goal as summer began? Avoiding Mr. G.

He spent much of the day indoors during winter. But in the summer, there he was, out by the giant oak tree in the front yard. A long, rutted dirt road expanded behind it, back to a field gone fallow, eventually to some piney woods. We really wanted to scope out those woods. But there was no way we could with Mr. G there. Not that we didn't try.

One time, we crept along the steep bank stretching along his property down to the tracks. Nobody kept the briars in check here. Later in the summer, that meant fat blackberries, big as your thumb. For now, the brambles created an impenetrable barrier that some spell surely required to break through. We found that if we followed alongside the property long enough in this thicket, we could get to the piney woods. Mr. G would never know.

But those briars were too dang thick.

One day, Jay and I left my house, and were walking out to the curve of road that stretched across the rickety wooden railroad bridge. We yammered on about Transformers, heedless of anything else save the heat that struck us. The skin under our eyes even sweated. We had just about turned the corner of my property's fence to go to Jay's when someone hollered at us.

We stopped dead. Oh God! Mr. G.

If I had liked Jay as more than a friend, I would have pressed against him. But we weren't close like that. So we stared at each other. I could almost read his mind: "Let's run."

Yet for some reason, I turned back and dared to look across the road. Mr. G leaned against his great oak tree, next to his screened-in shed.

It was too late to run then.

Mr. G said, "Come on over here!"

I heard Jay whimper.

But I was too curious now. What did this Guardian of the Piney Woods want? The adventurer in me took charge.

"Let's go," I whispered, without moving my lips. Just in case.

We looked left and right, and then dashed across the pavement. Our feet met the mix of red dirt and gravel of Mr. G's farm road. We advanced slowly to him.

I could then make out the colors of the shed better. He had once painted it bright red, but now its color was faded from the unpredictable Tennessee weather over the years.

We faced him. And we, at ten and eleven years old, were surprisingly Mr. G's height. He was stooped, we discovered. His pale blue, rheumy eyes wheeled slightly in different directions. He smiled a toothless grin.

"I've got something for you," he rasped.

And Jay looked at me, and we both thought, "He's gonna murder us."

But I swallowed and squeaked.

He went into his shed, and neither of us followed. But we didn't have to. Mr. G soon returned. He held in his hands a pile of lollipops with their wrappers on. Pristine.

He said, "Here you go!"

We hesitated. And he laughed at us!

"Now, don't be afraid. I seen y'all playin' around down by the track. You can play over here all you want. I don't do nothin' unless the tobacco needs cuttin'. Most of the time I just nap."

We were astounded. And I asked the burning question.

"Can we play in those woods back there?"

Mr. G cackled. "Sure, sure. But whenever you do, you have to stop by for a lollipop first!"

And from then on, Mr. G became our friend, and that was the best summer.

SOURWOOD HONEY DAYS

You could tell when it was sourwood honey time. The valleys curled listlessly between the ancient mountains, redolent in honeysuckle and black locust blossoms. Everyone in the lowlands lived in a kind of torpor. It was almost July, and you could feel it under your eyelids, the sweat making its way in crevices you didn't want it to. You'd push the sweat off your brow and look up at the smoke-blue smudge of undulation on the horizon. The mountains! They called to us all.

Back in the day, the highlands were a resort area. Places like Maggie Valley and Blowing Rock drew folks out of their sultry homes from flatter and hotter climes. There weren't any good interstates up in the mountains back then. So you'd snake your way on twisty mountain roads. And if you were lucky, by God, there'd be a sourwood honey stand on the side of the road.

Dad favored Grandfather Mountain for the honey stands. Up that twisty road of switchbacks, I had to keep swallowing and trying to find the horizon, before the road made me sick. I carried my little headset radio with me, and you could pick up all sorts of stations in the mountains. I was listening to Asheville, North Carolina! They sure had a better selection than East Tennessee when it came to music.

The farther up the road we went, the foggier it became. The temperature plummeted, but my excitement grew. I could feel it: we were almost there. And then, sure enough, the spray of gravel as Dad turned the car off the side of the road and parked next to our quarry.

Ramshackle little roadside markets with rows of deep amber-hued liquid in jars. Sourwood honey! The legend, the only one! Jars clear, jars translucent…Dad went for the latter, because those held honeycomb. He liked to eat the comb. There was really something about seeing those jars that sent a thrill through me. To think that bees that only favored sourwood tree blossoms could make that tangy-sweet elixir…surely that was mountain magic.

Jars purchased, we headed back down the mountain. Then we could open our jars over time and think back to sourwood honey days. We drizzled the bees' quarry over our buttered biscuits and waited for the weather in the lowlands to cool down. There is no honey like sourwood honey, the jewel of the highlands.

TRACKS iN AUTUMN

Autumn on the tracks at Gray. Sunlight slanting amber, gilding twin streams of silver line destined for coalfields in blue mountains. I remember gossamer summer warmth, a few katydids, and grasshoppers singing last call. Sumac turning. Pokeweed jutting out of blackberry bushes that gave forth their bounty two months before.

The smell of sweet hay, like bread baking.

Moon hanging in the sky, misty, a vision and not at all real.

Walking along, skipping over the wooden ties, or balancing on the line. I knew the trick to that. You step on, one foot before the other, and gaze some twenty feet down the line. You walk and never look at your feet.

Creosote. Thick like the blood of the tracks. For they do live. They throb, they groan, they buckle and screech. That is why I treat them with respect. Old glass knobs, rusty spikes, bones of dead animals.

Shimmering heat above the black-stained ties, even this late in the year.

I'm alone, of course. It's after dinner: roast beef with potatoes and carrots, a pat of butter on my roll, Sprite to drink.

I dash down the red clay grade. Dirt all over me, of course. It doesn't matter. I wear the gossamer summer on this stretch of the line like royal robes of pure topaz.

Written August 25, 2000.

RESONANT THOUGHTS

SOME POETRY

ODE TO ACER SACCHARUM

Splendid-leaved
Fire
Sugar
Water
Brilliant hands that fall
Drift onto my face
Coloring my dreams
Torch-light trees,
Boastful
Unabashed
Amber
Scarlet
Green-gold
Auburn
Spread before me
On wrinkled paper
My brush tracing shapes;
Liquid dreams,
Heady-sweet
Love dreamt of
Love fallen
As your leaves
In Autumn.

APPALACHIA

The air hands with honeysuckle
It splits with lightning
And grumbles with thunder.

The land gathers folds around itself
And squeezes out streams of tears
To cascade or wander.

The water cloaks the hills or
Douses the valleys in torrents
And drapes its fog down yonder.

Home it is, a different air
I breathe today, and land I
Step upon and with tears, I ponder.

Written December 19, 2002, in Seattle, Washington. I sent this to Ursula K. Le Guin and she responded in a letter to me.

THE YULE STAG

There is a hush on winter nights
That glisten in frost
And the dripping remnants
Of a recent snowmelt
Stand still, and gleam
In the light of a full moon.

The softest footfalls
Stir the stillness,
And lo,
A lone stag wanders
Among the firs
Amidst the holly.

Who knows where
He has come from.
Does he have
A family?
These mysteries
Remain unknown.

But he is generous,
He stands ready
To guide you
Through the moonlit paths
And the soft shadows cast
On this cold winter night.

OBSIDIAN

I hold within
My weathered hands
A heavy weight
Etched and curved
Once sand, burned
In volcanic fire
Made anew as
Black glass
And this I hold,
This you did to me.

Ancient remnant
My caress of you
Hands within
Hands without
Enclosed inside
This hard and
Colorless void
Once new as
Liquid flame
And this I grieve
This you took from me.

Struck upon
My flinted heart
Darkened blades
Darker thoughts
Darkling shards
From magma, knives
Whet now as
This time

And this I bear:
I cut my thoughts from thee.

A CURSED GOBLET

Drink of this
Blessed elixir
Whence clouds of hornets whirl
Pierce your throat
Collapse your resolve
Drink deeply, dear girl.

Did you assume,
Gilded cypher,
That your acts might slither
Through my briars?
Forsake your bravado:
Send your courage hither.

Come closer,
Stammering princess,
Of bent and sundered crown!
Cease your sobs
Falter your footsteps
May your blood run down!

Drink of this
Poisoned goblet
Noisome and full of reek
Choke your lungs!
Dissolve your freedom!
I have rendered you weak.

PUBLICATION HISTORY

One Evening in Fogvale: original to this collection

The Night of Longshanks: San Diego Writers and Editors Guild anthology *The Power of Ten*, 2021

A Hard Landing: Queen Mob's Tea House, February 2019

Overdue in Deep Space: original to this collection

Void Mage: original to this collection

The Scaffold: original to this collection

Roder: original to this collection

Topaz Sundered: original to this collection

Blue Lantern Nightfall: previously published on Medium

Galleon's Wake: original to this collection

The Tunnel at the End: previously published on Medium

Stolen Art: previously published on Medium

Autumn's Dusk: original to this collection

The Glove and the Black Lantern: original to this collection

The River of Rubies: original to this collection

Valentines from the Pit: previously published on Medium

Screens in Between: previously published on Medium

The Queen and the Mountain Laurel: original to this collection

Mister Gerald: previously published on Medium

Sourwood Honey Days: previously published on Medium

Tracks in Autumn: original to this collection

Ode to *Acer Saccharum*: original to this collection

Appalachia: original to this collection

The Yule Stag: previously published on Medium

Obsidian: original to this collection

A Cursed Goblet: original to this collection

ACKNOWLEDGMENTS

Years ago, on cold winter nights, when the stars burned in tiny, distant fires above my rural East Tennessee home, Dad would get out an old telescope he built, and his binoculars, and show me the universe. I grew fond of the constellations, and daydreamed about the stars within them, and whether they had worlds spinning around them. I even formed an astronomy club for my young friends, and speculated in my newsletters about those exoplanets.

My father is gone now, but he has rejoined the stars above, and now we know there are indeed exoplanets beyond count. Dad instilled in me a love for science, nature, and also for writing…for he was a writer himself. He was a teller of tall tales, a global traveler, a writer of novels, short stories, and poetry. My mother worked for a printing press and had a keen eye for editing. Between those two parents, of course, I was destined to become a writer. I thank both my parents for their encouragement and help over the years.

I wrote whenever I could put pen to paper, which was often, and I drew in the margins and outside of them. I always told stories to anyone who would listen. And I appreciate everyone who did, or pretended they did. I'm grateful to everyone who has supported my writing journey, from my 8th grade teacher who wrote to publishing companies on my behalf in the late 1980s, to the writing communities I've found and fostered both online and out in the world.

I am most grateful to my beloved Gareth L. Powell, a fellow writer and a brilliant one, for his unwavering belief in me and his unconditional love. I love you, Gareth.

I would like to thank my editors Scarlett R. Algee and Sean Leonard of JournalStone/Trepidatio for polishing THE SHADOW GALAXY collection, and for Scarlett's belief in this book.

There are many writers and friends to thank as well. First, my supporters, Carrie Ancell, Michael Mulhern, Bradley Nordell, Alex Bird Tillson, Robert Young, Richard Czernik, Carter Allen, Lorraine Grant, Robyn Lynn Taylor, Louise Murphy, Rich Curtis, Angela Blackwell, David Perlmutter, Melissa Davis, and Nick Steffensmeier.

Thank you to my writing friends Mya Duong, Jonathan Maberry, Bonnie Burton, Adrian Tchaikovsky, Diane Duane, Jody Houser, Rachael Smith, Paul Cornell, Lizbeth Myles, Sophia McDougall, Mike Chen, Lou Anders, Flo McGrath, Noah Kinsey, Tade Thompson, Lee Harris, Melissa F. Olson, Geoff Ryman, Tone Milazzo, Melissa Milazzo, Eddie Robson, Sarah Miles, Tori Eldridge, Greg Van Eekhout, Lisa Will, Henry L. Herz, Austin Farmer, Dennis K. Crosby, Karama Horne, Erika Ensign, Jackson Lanzing, Dani Colman, Carolyn Hinds, Brian Schirmer, C.E. Murphy, Ren Hutchings, James Moran, Antony Johnston, C. Robert Cargill, Aliette de Bodard, Jess Capelle, Danika K. Stone, James Jensen, Premee Mohamed, Seth Lukas Hynes, Cory Doctorow, S.B. Divya, Alex Segura, Jonathan L. Howard, John Scalzi, and Chuck Wendig.

Thank you to exceptionally supportive friends Pam and Hector Magnus and Jessica Springer.

This collection of short stories and poetry includes tales written decades ago and some quite recent. This is an intensely personal set of works, showcasing different genres, and proving that we cannot have a shadow without light as well.

ABOUT THE AUTHOR

J. Dianne Dotson is a science fiction, fantasy, and horror author of THE SHADOW GALAXY: A Collection of Short Stories and Poetry (March 3, 2023, from Trepidatio Publishing) as well as the four-book space opera series THE QUESTRISON SAGA® (*Heliopause*; *Ephemeris*; *Accretion*; and *Luminiferous*).

Dianne dreamed up other worlds and their characters as a child in the 1980s in East Tennessee. She formed her own neighborhood astronomy club before age 10, to educate her friends about the universe. In addition to writing stories, she drew and painted her characters, designed their outrageous space fashions, and created travel guides and glossaries for the worlds she invented.

Dianne's short fiction is featured in anthologies and magazines. She holds a degree in Ecology and Evolutionary Biology and spent several years working in both ecological and clinical research. Dianne is also a science writer for online publications. She is known for writing characters people fall in love with, in extraordinary settings with intricate world-building. Dianne is also an artist.

As a convention guest, Dianne provides insight into science fiction writing and characters (featured at Star Wars Celebration, San Diego Comic-Con, WonderCon, Cymera Festival in Scotland, and BristolCon in England), the science of science fiction films, and offers lectures on writing and world-building at conventions and universities.

Dianne is a member of the Science Fiction Writers Association, the Horror Writers Association, the British Science Fiction Association, and the British Fantasy Society. She lives with her family in Los Angeles, California, and in Bristol, England, and is married to British science fiction author Gareth L. Powell.

CPSIA information can be obtained
at www.ICGtesting.com
Printed in the USA
BVHW030347170223
658574BV00012B/138